CRASH-LANDING

Where was he?

The Revelation crashed on a small, unknown planet—the spacecraft is disabled. Trist finds the natives have no technology. They are ignorant, brutish people constantly fighting other warriors called—Romans.

He takes a long-sleep pill to escape to another time, hoping to awake in a more civilized era. He wakes to see the girl, Selena.

Why leave?

Other Books By Michael Elder:

FLIGHT TO TERROR
NOWHERE ON EARTH
PARADISE IS NOT ENOUGH
THE ALIEN EARTH

THE ALIEN EARTH

by Michael Elder

PINNACLE BOOKS • NEW YORK CITY

THE ALIEN EARTH

Copyright © 1971 by Michael Elder

A Pinnacle Books edition, published by special arrangement with Robert Hale & Company, London.

ISBN: 0-523-00829-5

First printing, July 1971
Second printing, March 1976

Cover illustration by Randy Weidner

Printed in the United States of America

PINNACLE BOOKS, INC.
275 Madison Avenue
New York, N.Y. 10016

THE ALIEN EARTH

PROLOGUE

If Greet had had his helmet on it might have been all right. But Greet had always been impetuous to the point of foolhardiness, and it was certainly easier to examine the *Revelation's* outer hull from the tiny scout ship if your vision wasn't hampered by a helmet.

And so Greet died and Trist lived.

When the alarm shrieked Trist's first reflex action was to slam shut his face-plate. Greet's normally cheerful face blanched at the noise and his hands clawed for his helmet on the couch beside him. Through his external mike Trist heard the harsh hiss of air escaping from the scout ship, and it seemed only a matter of seconds before the hiss faded and vanished and he knew the scout ship was in vacuum.

He felt Greet's gloved hand clutch desperately at his wrist, and then the grip slackened. Trist stared at him and then hastily turned away. He had no wish to be sick locked in his space suit.

He would have to get back to the cruiser quickly. His suit had only an hour's worth of oxygen. He glanced out of the wide forward viewport and blinked in disbelief. The *Revelation* had hung there a few moments ago, almost close enough to touch. Now it had gone.

Perhaps whatever had hit the scout ship had swung them off course, and Trist turned to the console to try to locate the *Revelation* on the radar screen, his mind already wondering why, if they had been pushed off course, there had been no radio message from the cruiser. Normally Captain Graud would have been roaring at them to adjust their course within seconds, but in fact since the scream of the alarm had died in the suddenly created vacuum there had been an ominous silence from his suit radio.

So far he had not panicked. Greet's death had been quick and horrible, but any crewman on a deep-space ship lived with this possibility always in the back of his mind. The procedure since the alarm had been routine for self-defence. Now, however, as he looked at the console he felt the first exploratory movement of icy fingers down his spine and his heart stuttered.

There was no sign of the *Revelation* on the radarscope. And the speed reading was well into the red.

Instinctively he glanced out of the viewport. Nothing. Nothing except an impenetrable, meaningless blackness. But he had surpassed the speed of light, and even as he punched the braking engines he told himself that the scientists were wrong. Ships surpassing the speed of light disappeared, not unnaturally, since no instruments could then detect them. Scientists had assumed that ships going superlight disintegrated, for none had ever reappeared.

Well, he had not disintegrated. He was still in one somewhat battered piece, but the battering had taken place before they went superlight, and so far as he could tell they had suffered no further damage since.

But Trist would not be able to tell the scientists they were wrong. Unless his was to be the exception and become the first ship to come back again. Grimly he told himself that he had joined the select company of perhaps a dozen ships which had vanished without trace, a distinction he would willingly have foregone.

He watched dully as the needle dropped out of the red area of danger and the stars winked back into view. He sighed with relief. He was still alive and he was perhaps the first person to have come back from

8

travelling past the light barrier.

But his relief was short lived. A quick study of the stars outside showed them to be strange, patterned in unknown configurations, mysterious and unconcerned, remote, except for one much closer than the others, almost straight ahead of him through the viewport.

The strangeness hit him like a hammer blow and his head reeled with an awful feeling of disorientation.

Where was he?

The disappearance of earlier superlight ships crowded his mind as he searched the unfamiliar backdrop. Where had they gone and, what was more terrifying, why had they not come back? Had they entered some strange parallel universe, alien and uninhabited by creatures such as they, and was that where he was now, alone and totally lost?

Panic welled in him and he fought it down. If he gave way to it he would surely die. If he kept control he might not.

That one close star seemed to beckon him and for a while he stared in its direction, wondering. He had nothing to lose. The scout ship seemed to be heading straight for it and grimly he began to check the console.

The cabin was drained of oxygen. He had perhaps forty-five minutes' supply in his suit pack, and suddenly he cursed and leant over to the still form on the couch beside him. He turned off the suit oxygen from Greet's pack. It must have been leaking steadily into the vacuum since the accident, and Greet had no need of it now. That would give him an extra forty-five minutes. Though what use an extra forty-five minutes was going to be in this situation he couldn't imagine.

What had caused the accident?

The *Revelation* had passed through a meteor shower and once they were through Captain Graud had ordered Greet and Trist out in the scout ship to check for damage to the cruiser's corenium plates. And it was more than likely that while they were out a meteor bringing up the rear of the shower had collided with them, tearing a hole in the cabin and opening the main engine throttles. The scout ship, which had been matching the sublight speed of the *Revelation* had streaked through the light barrier.

But this was only of academic interest. Within the next hour and a half he must find out where he was and how he was going to be rescued.

True, he had the sleep pills, which were standard equipment on scout ships, if all else failed. If an accident happened a sleep pill would put the pilot and co-pilot to sleep until they were rescued, a deep sleep during which they needed no food, no water and no air. With ships unable to travel faster than light crews finding themselves in this situation might have to wait a long time for rescue and reawakening. Trist had no idea how long the effects of the sleep pill lasted. He doubted if anyone had had to sleep long enough to find out.

And he doubted if he would find out now. The pills were in the emergency locker, one for the pilot, one for the co-pilot. He only had to reach out a hand for one. But between his mouth and his hand was the face-plate of his helmet and a lot of vacuum . . .

He switched the radio to the general distress frequency.

"Scout ship Two to *Revelation*. Scout ship Two to *Revelation*. Come in, please."

He held his breath, listening to his suit speaker, but there was nothing except the distant steady mush of the stars.

"Scout Ship Two to any ship. Scout Ship Two to any ship. This is a Grade One emergency. Come in, please."

He repeated his message again and again, and then switched off quickly. He felt panic rising at the silence which greeted him, the silence of endless distances of emptiness.

Where was the *Revelation?* He had only been faster than light for a few moments, and not much faster, either. If he had gone in and out so quickly he ought still to be within radio range.

But if he had gone in and out so quickly the star patterns would never have changed as drastically as they had done . . ..

There was something here he did not understand.

He felt the sweat forming on his forehead and he forced himself to keep calm. The fact must be faced realistically.

He was lost. Beyond the reach of help from his own world. And with the acceptance of that fact Haven suddenly seemed infinitely desirable, a place of bright sunshine and warmth and friendliness and his heart ached with a desperate homesickness.

Stop that, he thought. *Self pity won't help.*

He touched the braking engines again, for the needle was once more creeping up towards the red. The meteor must have jammed the main engine throttles open and he would need to watch the speed all the time in case they went superlight again. But there couldn't be much fuel left for the engines now. They had almost completed their survey of the *Revelation* when the accident happened and the engines must have used a lot since. Once that had gone he would be helpless, a tiny bubble marooned in a vast and hostile void.

The star he had seen earlier was very much larger now, and would soon be too bright to look at without shading his face-plate. It was a star very similar to Haven's primary, and he wondered if there was any possibility that it had a system. And if it had, would it have a planet which might support life?

He shied at the idea as though the mere thought was enough to make a planetary system vanish. But it would not die. It was the only thing left to cling to, so he punched the radarscope for close scan, and immediately there were bodies stretching out from the star. One, two, three, four big ones and several smaller ones. He was very close to the outermost of the big planets.

He scanned the console again. The broken fuel gauge had registered zero ever since the accident, so he had no way of judging what he had in reserve, but it couldn't be much. He had little or no time for a proper survey. The four big planets he rejected immediately. They were too far out from the primary and gravity would make them uninhabitable if nothing else did. Somewhere between the biggest of these four and the primary itself there might possibly be a world small enough not to crush him and warm enough to live on.

He made a quick decision and switched off the main engines. If he found a suitable world he would need all the fuel in the smaller braking engines to control his altitude and to slow him sufficiently to land. The main engines died so he switched the fuel feeds to the braking engines. Now he was committed. If this failed he could never restart the main engines. He could never leave this system without getting out and giving the scout ship a major overhaul which he doubted his ability to perform. But then what did it matter? If this idea failed there was nowhere else for him to go.

The steady hiss of oxygen suddenly stuttered. The pack was empty. He switched his suit tube to Greet's supply, murmuring a word of apology as he did so but carefully avoiding looking at the distorted face behind the half replaced helmet.

Now he had forty-five minutes of oxygen.

And after that, nothing.

It was a perfect world, cloud-flecked and a brilliant blue. It looked too good to be true. Third from the primary and with an abnormally large satellite. Trist bit his lip as he felt the first tug of the atmosphere press

12

him into his couch. What did that atmosphere consist of? He had no idea and he would have no idea until he summoned up the courage to remove his helmet and take a deep breath, for the meters which should monitor external pressure and atmosphere content were dead.

The pressure built up as the scout ship came in. Soon he heard the roaring hiss of atmosphere entering the cabin through the hole torn by the meteor and the internal air meter began to tremble and climb slowly round its dial.

Below him the world spun closer. The white of cloud and the green of land. The deep blue of oceans and the light of the primary sparkling and winking on the water. Trist felt himself smiling. It looked good. Surely it must be livable in. Nowhere could look as beautiful as this and yet be deadly.

He could hear the braking engines whine when he touched the switches and the scout ship floated down as the world spun below. A huge land mass glided past and away, and the blue sparkle of water was under them now. Trist stopped the braking engine to let the scout ship glide on. It would be a sad thing at this stage to bring the ship down on water and then drown.

The water seemed to go on for a long time as the ship drifted lower and for a while Trist worried that he would not be able to maintain sufficient height until land appeared beneath them again. With the main engines dead he could not gain altitude.

Then land, and he braked again. The scene below slowed its headlong flow. A strip more water, but not much this time, and then more land, and Trist brought the braking engines to full power.

Green hills and brown plains, warm in the glow of the primary. Winding rivers and plentiful vegetation, strange shadowy cloud shapes gliding over the land.

He killed three of the braking engines and the scout

13

ship turned until Trist was facing the incredible blue of the sky out of which he had just come. Then all four engines again as the gravity of the planet pulled the ship towards it and he compensated for the pull as well as he could.

Outside he saw the peak of a hill spread upwards over the viewport. He seemed to be coming down frighteningly fast into a valley and he gave a last desperate burst of engine power. There was a crash and he felt himself pressed hard into his couch. The scout ship seemed to bounce upwards and then settle again. Through his helmet he heard a rending, scraping sound. The ship lurched and shuddered, slipped and twisted. He heard things scrape sharply at the viewpoints, but it seemed to be nothing but the branches of vegetation. A sudden thump, harder than any so far, and then there was silence.

Trist flicked off the engines and flexed his hands, feeling the dampness of his palms soaking into the absorbent material of his suit gloves.

Beside him Greet had slipped and was now lying on his side as though he had turned over in his sleep.

Trist listened. There was no sound except for the gentle hiss of oxygen feeding his suit from Greet's pack. The internal air meter on the console had climbed well within the acceptable tolerance, though it was lower than it would have been on Haven. But that did not mean the atmosphere was breathable . . .

There was no point in waiting. The sooner he knew the better.

He raised his hands and began to unclamp the fastenings of his faceplate.

ONE

1

The Legate stood at the window of the Commandant's house and looked out at the glistening roadstones of the fort and the bleak grey of the hills beyond the walls. The scar where he had been struck a glancing blow by a Pictish spear years before had turned a fiery red, as it always did when he was tired and uncertain. A gnarled finger nervously traced its furrow.

"I'm too old for war, Marcus," he said querulously. "I used to think it was glorious. Now it just seems messy. It was easier when I was younger. We had the strength to keep the peace then, and a man had his own gods and could worship as he pleased. Ever since the old Emperor took to this Christianity it's been nothing but trouble, trouble, trouble."

He turned faded blue eyes and looked at the younger man sitting on the heavy plain wooden chair. Marcus looked back at the Legate calmly. Neither resembled the old idea of the masters of the world, members of the ruling Roman Empire. Two hundred years ago this fort of Cilurnum had been a thriving place, alive with the shouts of men and the jingling harness of the cavalry legion which had manned this section of the Wall. There had been a glory and a purpose then which had shown the local tribes that the Romans were here to impose their peace and civilization on them. But it was a far outpost of the Empire, and that civilization had never been more than skin deep.

Times had changed since then. The Wall still stood, but the great legions had gone to fight battles nearer home. Those tribesmen who had become Romanized

15

by marriage and by usage were left as best they could to man the Wall themselves and to keep out the barbarians who lived in the wilderness beyond.

Much of the Roman civilization had inevitably disappeared. Frequent attacks by the Picts on the Wall made it unsafe for a man to live outside the fort. Too often his crops were burnt, his wife raped and his children killed, and now those members of the Romanized tribe of the Brigantes who were unfortunate enough to live within range of the Wall sheltered in the fort itself, which had originally housed the barracks and stables of the great Second Asturians. There were no horses now. The stables were used as dormitories, and only the gateway to the south was kept open.

The Legate, whose title was a courtesy one, for he had no legion to command, brought himself back to the present with a start.

"You think an attack is coming?" he asked.

Marcus nodded. He was a small, wiry man with a nut brown face half hidden behind a tangle of thick black beard. His eyes were dark and surrounded by deep wrinkles. He could have been any age between twenty-five and fifty, but the Legate knew he was almost exactly between the two.

"I'm certain," he said.

"But where?"

Marcus shrugged and the skin cloak slipped from his narrow shoulders. He hitched it up again, for the room was cold. Perhaps the underfloor heating was still in working order, but there was no fuel for the fire, and the damp drizzle of the northern hills had seeped into his bones these last days.

"How can one tell?" he said.

"I must know," said the Legate. "It's all very well saying we may expect an attack, but where? The Wall is eighty miles long. We can't defend the entire length."

Marcus sighed.

"Listen," he said. "I've told you all I can. The Picts are preparing for trouble. In all the years I've gone trading north of the Wall this is the first time they have refused to barter. Usually they're only too keen to exchange their skins and hides for good food and grain. Now they don't seem to want any. And why? Because they *know* they needn't part with their skins. They *know* that very soon they'll have all the grain they want for the taking. And how are they going to get it? By taking it from us. Therefore they're preparing to attack."

The Legate turned back to the window and looked out again. The rain was still falling in the same relentless drizzle as though it never meant to stop.

"But where?" he muttered. "Here? Or at Luguvallum? Or at Segedunum? Or somewhere in between? I must know . . ." His fingers drummed nervously on the stone window sill. "There's no other reason they might not want your grain? Have they learnt to grow their own?"

Marcus shook his head.

"If they had they would have told me. But they didn't. In any case they didn't make me welcome. I was glad to get back to Cilurnum without a spear in my back. No, there's something afoot, Legate."

The Legate nodded gloomily.

"I think you're right," he said. "There's been an ominous quiet on the Wall for some time. Oh, people have said the Picts have decided to leave us alone, but I know that's not true. And if they catch us unprepared we could be overrun." He turned suddenly to Marcus. "You see that, don't you?" he asked.

"I see that," said Marcus quietly.

"Our lives may depend on foreknowledge. If we know where and when the attack will come we can draw men from other fronts to meet it. We may be able to drive them back with such losses that they will think seriously about attacking the Wall again. At least for a while. And that may give Rome time to remember us and perhaps send help. If they ever clear up this question of which god they expect us all to worship."

Marcus stood up and began pacing backwards and forwards across the room with its low arches and small rounded windows. At one time, it was said, this had been a handsome, comfortable room, furnished with colorful hangings by the Commandant's wife, full of rich furniture from the heartland of the Empire. That had all gone now. It was cold and bare and draughty. The glory and the triumph had disappeared along with the splendid furnishings, strangled by the unconquerability of the wilderness north of the Wall. Even the great Agricola had not been able to hold the northern lands, and in his day nearly three hundred years before there had been men to spare for conquest. But the hardy northern tribes had been too stubborn to subdue for long, and though the knowledge of Roman civilization and Roman law had spread far to the north it had been brief and spasmodic and the tribes had never accepted it. When Hadrian became Emperor the Wall was built to mark the limit of Roman government.

The trouble was that no one really understood the northern tribes. They were secretive and aloof. Marcus knew them as well as any man of the Romanised people south of the Wall. From years of trading with them, of bargaining skins for food, he had come to understand a small part of their culture and their make-up. But there was always a barrier. He was an outsider, one not accepted by the tribes, and though they usually greeted him with a kind of frigid formality and there existed between them a reluctantly cautious respect, he never got to know them as people. Their code of conduct and their beliefs were largely a mystery to him.

"The tribes seem—more united than usual," he said. "The Selgovae and the Votadini have got together. And

I have a feeling that there were some Damnonii near Trimontium. That's unusual."

"Very," said the Legate uneasily. "One of the reasons for our continued safety has been that they are almost always at loggerheads. What has brought them together?"

"I suppose they might have united in a common hatred of us and the Wall," said Marcus. "That's always been a possibility, though it's hard to understand what can have brought it to a head now rather than a hundred years ago."

The Legate frowned and nervously fingered the puckered scar on his cheek again. Then he nodded with a lot more briskness than he had shown before.

"If they unite they can destroy us," he said. "Maybe they have just realised that. There's only one thing to do."

Marcus raised his eyebrows.

"And what's that?" he asked.

"You will have to go back," said the Legate, and Marcus stared at him. He opened his mouth to protest, but the Legate cut him short. "Listen," he said. "You are the only one of us at Cilurnum with enough knowledge of the Picts to do the job. You know them, and they know you."

"That's ridiculous," said Marcus heatedly. "I've only just got back in one piece and they made it very clear they didn't want to see me again. If I go back now I certainly won't return alive."

The Legate laid a soothing hand on his shoulder.

"Then you will have to go secretly. I don't mind how you do it. Take a prisoner and bring him back for questioning—"

"That's no good. You know they won't talk."

"Then listen to what they say. You speak the language—"

"I can't go back—"

19

"But find out what's going on."

"I won't—"

"Marcus."

"What?"

"You agree that we must know?"

"Well—"

"You agree that if we don't know we could be overrun and butchered by the savages?"

"It's possible—"

"But that if we were forewarned we could be able to prevent it?"

"You may be right, but—"

"Can you suggest anyone else who could do the job, Marcus?"

"Oh, Jupiter—! All right! You leave me no choice. I'll go. But I won't go alone."

"Take anyone you want."

"I want Lucius. He's as tough as an ox, and if we get into a tight corner he may be able to get us out. If he can't no one can. And if there are two of us it doubles the chances of someone getting back with the information."

"Good. I knew you would see sense."

For a moment Marcus looked as if he might explode with anger, but he controlled himself and, not trusting himself to speak, he turned and left the room without a word, leaving the Legate standing at the window, his drawn face grey with worry, while the rain still fell outside.

2

It was still raining as Marcus and Lucius left the fort by the south gateway, and the darkness was almost complete. Here and there the dim glow of rushlights bloomed from the windows of the stables just inside the south gateway, but the little settlement outside the walls was silent and dark. Few people spent the night out here now, especially so late in the year as this.

Marcus led the way eastwards along the wall of the fort and down the slope, past the bath house to the bank of the river. There they turned upstream and could just make out the spans of the bridge carrying the Wall across the river and continuing up the slope of the far bank.

Marcus slipped off his deerskin shoes and lowered himself gently into the water, restraining a gasp as the icy current swirled round his legs and drove the breath from his body. The rains of the last few days had raised the level of the river quite a lot, and even at the bank here it came above his knees.

Behind him he heard Lucius stumble and splash and give vent to an oath. He turned quickly and shushed him.

Lucius's deep voice rumbled softly back at him.

"Don't understand why you can't go out the north gateway if you want to go north. Waste of time, this. Damned uncomfortable, too."

"They may be watching the gateways," whispered Marcus. "We must get well north of the Wall without being seen."

Lucius grunted and followed Marcus as he felt his way slowly under the arch of the bridge.

For all his taciturnity there was something very comforting about having Lucius with him. Many times when he had been at Cilurnum Marcus had watched Lucius as he went about his work repairing a wall or replacing a worn section in a house, effortlessly lifting huge blocks of stone which would have set a normal-sized man's bones cracking. Lucius moved with a slow deliberation and a steady inevitability and Marcus, whose work sometimes took him into unexpectedly tense situations, had often felt the man's company might be very useful.

21

And this crazy venture might well call for physical violence before it was finished.

The rippling water of the river seemed louder as it echoed round the stonework of the arch and then faded as they worked clear. Marcus clenched his teeth and continued to wade against the freezing water until they were past the northern ditch which formed the Wall's first line of defense.

Some distance beyond, where the river chuckled shallowly over a long ridge of stones, he turned and led Lucius across by a makeshift ford and gained the far bank.

They stood there for a while, trying to dry their feet and stamp some semblance of feeling back into their numbed limbs. The rain still drizzled down relentlessly, and already the outline of the Wall was lost behind them in the darkness. Marcus sat down and drew his shoes on over his still wet feet. He shivered. They were alone in the wilderness.

For a man who spent a large part of his life amongst the northern tribes this reaction seemed odd, but he realized that it was the first time he had come north carrying a spear and a short sword instead of goods to barter.

"Come," he said, and stood up.

Lucius swore, but Marcus saw the huge form stir and get to his feet, and a few moments later they set off again, Marcus leading. He had no stars to guide him, but he knew that if he kept the sound of the river within earshot he would be heading in the right direction.

Behind him he could hear Lucius padding steadily over the soggy undergrowth of the river bank. The big man's presence was indeed a comfort.

When Marcus had stopped Lucius outside the old headquarters building the day before and asked him to come north beyond the Wall, Lucius had dusted his hands down his leather apron and fixed Marcus with a suspicious eye.

"What for?" he had asked, and nodded slowly and thoughtfully when Marcus explained, straightaway admitting the importance of the information they would be seeking.

"I'll come," he said. "How do we find out?"

"I don't know," Marcus admitted. "I have contacts. Maybe we would make use of them. But we may learn things simply by keeping our eyes and ears open."

"All right," said Lucius.

And here they were, soaked to the skin, shivering with the cold already a mile deep into the northern territory and still he had no clear plan of campaign. It was a mad escapade. If he could discover nothing when he had been accepted amongst the northern tribes could he do so when he was here simply as a spy? How could he expect to learn the inner councils of their war bands?

He was roused from his thoughts by Lucius gripping his elbow.

"We're being followed," he rumbled softly.

Marcus stopped, but all he could hear, apart from his pounding heart, was the faint hiss of the rain and the rippling of the nearby river.

"How do you know?" he asked.

"I heard them. They've stopped."

"You're imagining things," said Marcus with more conviction than he felt.

The big man shook his head. Marcus could just make out the movement in the darkness. He thought furiously. If they had been spotted so soon it was bad, and he knew enough of the hunting tribes to realize that once they had caught a trail they were unlikely to be thrown off it again. There was little point in going on with the expedition in these circumstances. It would be better to make their way back to Cilurnum while it was still dark and try again some other time. He could almost hear the Legate saying that the information they were seeking was urgent, but Marcus could see no urgency in committing suicide.

"We'll go back," he murmured. "Can we get past them?"

"I don't know," said Lucius. "Now we know they're there, perhaps. Depends how many there are."

"We could cross the river again, but they would probably see us. You're sure they're there?"

"Sure."

Marcus gnawed a damp corner of his beard. The problem was that their pursuers were between them and the Wall.

"We'll try moving away from the river and cutting back in a wide circle," he whispered. "Keep absolutely quiet. We may get past them before they realize what we're doing."

Lucius grunted in disbelief, but there was nothing else to do. Marcus led the way quietly up the shallow bank away from the river. The trouble was the land round about was almost bare of vegetation and what there was had lost its greenery for the year, so there was little cover.

Marcus hoped his sense of direction was sure enough to enable them to regain the Wall. With no stars or moonlight to guide him it might be very difficult.

The gurgle of the river faded and died behind them and its passing seemed to be the final break with reality. Now there was nothing except the steady hiss of the falling rain and a narrow field of half-vision limited to perhaps four paces in front of them. There was no wind which they might be able to keep in the same quarter, and even the rain was dropping straight down without the suggestion of a slant to guide them.

Something loomed out of the rain ahead and slightly

to one side, and Marcus's hand rose with the spear in it, but it was only a rock, black and glistening against the greyer background of the turf. He breathed a heavy sigh and wished his heart would quiet. It was making so much noise it was impossible to listen.

He pressed on, hearing the grumbling breathing of Lucius just behind him.

This stretch of ground seemed to be pitted with rocks, black-hummocks, tall spindles every shape and variety, and with the constant necessity of stepping round them Marcus soon lost whatever sense of direction he had had. It was not long before he was forced to confess that he had no idea which way he was going.

He stopped in confusion, straining to see further through the darkness than was possible, listening with held breath, willing his heart to be quiet.

There was something wrong. His instinct was screaming a warning at him.

He tried to separate and identify each tiny sound, and realized that there was only one—the falling rain. The swish of his footsteps had stopped and the river had faded into silence. But a sound which should have been there was missing.

Lucius's grumbling breathing was no longer behind him.

He whirled round, biting off his automatic desire to shout the big man's name.

Lucius had gone. He had completely disappeared . . .

Marcus let his breath whistle out in fear and disbelief. If only there had been a cry or the sound of a scuffle it would have been easier to accept, but there had been nothing.

He began to retrace his steps, his spear poised and ready. Alone now on the dark moor, surrounded by who knew what barbarian tribesmen, he felt the age-old terror of open spaces rising in him, the pointless,

25

purposeless fear of unknown and unknowable evil spirits which could drive a man mad if he gave way to it. He felt his head reeling. The ground seemed to be slipping and spinning away from him, black rocks circling round his head, and he beat at his temple with his free hand to try to force reason to return.

Suddenly there was a point of sanity. On the ground was a lump which was not a rock. It was shaped differently and even in this darkness it was colored differently, and the spinning stopped and his reeling brain settled as his senses focused on this known factor.

It was Lucius, his massive form stretched out as though he were asleep.

Marcus knelt beside him and had just time to notice the ugly bulge on his temple when something exploded behind him and the world which had been dark for so long suddenly burst into brilliant light before fading into a darkness deeper than that which he had known before.

3

Marcus, on one of his trading trips many years before, had seen a Pictish coracle caught in a squall in the Bodotria Estuary. He had watched the frail craft being tossed on the rising waves as the fishermen tried to head for the shore, and he remembered marvelling at the way the coracle had ridden those terrifying seas and had eventually, through the moaning wind and the squally showers of rain, come safely to the beach.

He was in that craft now. For the first time he had personal experience of that crazy tossing backwards and forwards and sideways all at the same time, and he heard the moaning of the wind through the wickerwork of the coracle's hull.

For a moment he experienced to the full this strange sensation until suddenly its dreamlike quality evaporated and he knew that it was not the wind which was moaning but himself.

And with that realisation came the pain, and the moan turned into a scream. His wrists and ankles blazed with a searing agony which faded into a merciful and meaningless black jumble as he lost consciousness again.

The next he knew the coracle had gone, and everything was still. He immediately remembered the pain at his wrists and ankles, and although there was still a throb of discomfort the agony seemed to have stopped.

He opened his eyes cautiously and blinked in the unaccustomed glare of a watery sun newly risen above the eastern hills.

He was lying on his side on the ground, and just in front of his eyes lay a long pole to which his wrists were tied. Looking down the length of the pole he could see that his feet were lashed to the far end. There was sufficient length of pole beyond his feet and wrists to rest on the shoulders of a couple of carriers. Hence the sensation of being thrown about in a storm-swept coracle, and he understood the agony of that journey when he looked more closely at his wrists. The rough grass ropes had been drawn tight by his own weight. They had rubbed and chafed at the skin until it was red and raw, and the ropes themselves were stained dark with his blood.

The sight and the realization brought the pain pounding back up his arms and legs and he waited tensely for it to reach his head.

The red wave hit him and swamped him and he clenched his teeth not to cry out.

The wave passed, leaving him awash with a pulsing queasiness, but he was able to open his eyes again and see beyond the radius of his own wrists and ankles.

A cooking fire was burning some distance away and crouched over it were two small, wiry figures, one of whom, despite the bitter weather, wore only a loin cloth of animal skins. His body was covered with strange colored patterns. The other, wearing a body skin, had similar patterns daubed on his legs and arms.

These were the Picts, the painted people. Marcus recognised them as being of the Selgovae, the tribe he had often traded with in the past, though he did not recognise the individuals.

Where were they going? Why were they taking the trouble to carry him when they could quite easily have taken his spear and sword, cut his throat and left him for the crows to pick?

This action was highly uncharacteristic of the tribes.

The stark remains of a ruined wall and the configuration of the background hills told him where they were. This was Bremenium, once a fort of the Roman road to Trimontium in the days when the country had been occupied in strength at least as far north as Antoninus Pius's Wall. He had often passed the ruined fort on his journeys to barter with the tribes.

So their captors were taking them north.

Where was Lucius? Marcus felt a twinge of conscience that this was the first time he had recalled the big man whom he had last seen lying in the soaking ground unconscious at the least, and perhaps even dead.

He looked round as well as he could, moving his cramped and aching limbs gingerly, but he could see no sign of Lucius. His heart sank. Had he been left dead on the moor?

The two men at the fire paid no attention to him. He could hear the dull mutter of their voices as they worked, but they were too far away for him to make out what they were saying. There was little strength in the sun and although he was lying directly in its rays it

28

did nothing to warm him or ease the awful ache in his bones.

He dozed off, for how long he did not know, and when he opened his eyes a group of men was climbing the slope towards the fort from the line of the old road. His heart leapt as he recognized the central figure in the woven wool tunic, towering head and shoulders above the skin clad tribesmen.

Lucius seemed to be walking with difficulty and Marcus saw that his wrists and ankles too were raw and bleeding, though he must have managed to struggle to some water supply and wash them clean.

Lucius shuffled forward and stood looking down at him. There was an ugly blue bruise at his temple and his sword and spear had gone, but apart from that he looked the same huge, imperturbable character who might simply be preparing for another day's work repairing the walls of Cilurnum.

"How are you?" he asked.

"All right," said Marcus. "My wrists and ankles ache, but that's all."

"What do they want with us?"

"I don't know," said Marcus.

"Ask them," Lucius grunted. "You speak the language."

Marcus looked round at the four tribesmen who had taken up positions round him. There was no obvious leader so he asked them collectively where they were going. They stared at him for a minute and then one of them shrugged his shoulders, and the group turned away in silence.

Lucius grunted and knelt down, gently examining the wounds at Marcus's wrists and ankles. Even the softest touch was agony and Lucius grunted again, rose to his full height and called to the tribesmen. Something in the tone of his voice forced them to turn back, and Lucius made a sawing motion with his hand and pointed to

29

Marcus's bonds. There was a muttered consultation, and then one of the tribesmen stepped forward, produced a crude knife and knelt down.

He cut the ropes with unexpected gentleness. Marcus struggled to sit upright and tried to move his fingers, but the effort was too agonizing and he stopped. Lucius made washing gestures to the tribesmen. There was another consultation and then one of them left the group, leading down the slope from which Lucius had come.

There was silence while the remaining tribesmen stood staring unblinkingly at them until the fourth man returned with a pitcher of water, and a moment later there was a hail from one of the men at the fire, and the tribesmen turned to go and eat.

Lucius began to wash Marcus's torn wrists with a piece of his tunic.

"Strange people," he rumbled as he carefully wiped away the dried blood. "We're prisoners, yet they take our orders. This I do not understand."

The same thought had crossed Marcus's mind. Twice the tribesmen had done what Lucius had wanted, and it had not been done through fear of the big man's size.

"We are being treated with honor. Why?" asked Lucius.

"Maybe their king wants hostages," said Marcus doubtfully.

Lucius snorted and rinsed out the piece of cloth in the pitcher. The cool water was easing the pain in Marcus's wrists, but they were very raw, the flesh torn almost to the bone in some places."

"I think not," said Lucius. "Look at them closely."

Marcus did so, and noticed something which he had missed before. Two of the men had different patternings painted on their bodies and the pigments were not the same as those used by the others.

"Those men are Damnonii," he murmured. "The others are Selgovae."

"Is that what they are?" grunted Lucius. "I knew they were different."

"Selgovae and Damnonii in the one hunting party. It's unheard of."

"And why do they want us alive?"

Marcus shook his head as Lucius turned to his ankles and began to bathe them, his eyes constantly wandering in puzzlement to the oddly assorted group around the fire.

Some time later four of the tribesmen stretched themselves out beside the fire while the other two took up positions on nearby rocks where they could watch the approaches to the old fort and the prisoners at the same time, spears held loosely in their hands. Lucius took the hint and flopped down beside Marcus. In a few moments he was snoring heavily and very soon Marcus, overcome with weariness, followed his example.

4

They broke camp in mid-afternoon, and after a meal of a savory stew the fire was scattered and three of the tribesmen led the way down the slope ahead of Marcus and Lucius, while the other three brought up the rear.

The old road was overgrown and crumbling, but the line of it was still easily discernible, running straight as an arrow through the rough moorland on either side.

They were gaining height now, and the ramparts of hills ahead had a sprinkling of snow on their summits. Walking became difficult as their ankles stiffened, but their captors evidently wanted to clear the summit before nightfall and gave them no rest.

Soon Marcus had to concentrate on the physical effort of lifting one foot and placing it on the ground in

31

front of the other. He lost count of time and place, and was only vaguely aware that the watery sun had disappeared behind the hills to the west and that the thin drizzle of rain, now partly snow, had started once more.

They must have passed the summit without him realizing it, for suddenly he found that the road, rougher and more overgrown now, was running downhill between thick stands of trees.

As dusk fell they were halted and there was a muffled consultation amongst the tribesmen. Dimly Marcus felt that two of them wanted to press on to some further destination, while the other four wanted to stop here for the night. He found it difficult to follow the muttered, unaccustomed speech, but he did hear one voice raised in protest.

"The prisoners must be fresh when they arrive," it said, and vaguely Marcus wondered why the prisoners would have to be fresh . . .

This view seemed to prevail, for a few minutes later the tribesmen made camp in a clearing in the wood and soon a fire was burning, scattering the growing dusk and flickering redly on the trunks of the nearby trees.

They were given bowls of a hot broth to drink, and Marcus took his gratefully in trembling hands, feeling the welcome warmth thaw out frozen and cramped flesh, and soon after he fell into an exhausted and fitful doze.

The fire burnt low during the cold, dark hours, though Marcus was aware of the tribesmen feeding logs on to it occasionally. He lay between sleeping and waking most of the night, his teeth chattering and his limbs shaking uncontrollably. At one time he managed to crawl nearer the welcoming warmth of the fire. One of the tribesmen raised himself on an elbow to order him back, but after a look at Marcus's face he grunted and moved over to make room for him.

The warmth helped but he still could not sleep. Awful nightmares crowded in on him before he could drop off, nightmares in which he and Lucius were being prepared as a human sacrifice on a stone altar surrounded by thousands of savage tribesmen.

It may have been the dimly heard phrase about the prisoners having to be fresh which had impressed itself on his already fevered mind, but the waking nightmares were horribly real.

When dawn came he was weak and shivering and the amorphous nightmares seemed to have crystalised into some form of sense, though it was not a sense he cared to contemplate.

Lucius seemed to have recovered a lot during the night and managed to walk round with comparatively little discomfort, but Marcus found his own wrists and ankles badly swollen, and one ankle had begun to suppurate in a way which frightened him.

Lucius tried to bathe it for him, but it had become too sore to allow anyone to touch it, and with a grunt of concern he stopped trying and went to the fire and with gestures demanded food from the tribesmen who had finished eating and were preparing to strike camp.

Marcus managed to swallow a few mouthfuls of broth, but he had no appetite and he felt the first waves of fever sweep through him. It became urgent that he should communicate his reasoning of last night to Lucius before he became too delirious to do so.

"Listen, Lucius," he said through clenched teeth. "You know what we are, don't you?"

"Two fools who have walked into a trap of some sort," grunted Lucius.

"But you know what we are now?"

"What?"

"We're sacrifices."

Lucius turned to face him, his eyes calculating how much of this was due to fever.

33

"What makes you say that?" he asked.

"Why else should they take this trouble with us? Why should they want us fresh? Because we're butcher meat to them, that's why!"

Lucius considered for a while, working a morsel of gristle from the broth out of his teeth with his tongue.

"Maybe," he admitted at last.

"And if they're sacrificing us, they must be sacrificing us *to* something."

"That makes sense. So?"

Marcus paused as a fresh rigor swept through him.

"Something brought the tribes together," he gasped at last. "That's what our first worry was, remember? They've banded together to attack the Wall. What has brought them together? I'll tell you. It's the same thing that makes them want us for a sacrifice. They've found a new god."

Lucius glanced uneasily from Marcus to the tribesmen who were now gathering their few possessions and preparing to leave. There was a certain logic in what Marcus said, but precious little comfort. But there was no time to consider it further, for shortly afterwards they were following the old road again as it cut its way through the surrounding forest. Marcus managed to hobble with extreme difficulty for about a quarter of a mile, and then collapsed completely. The tribesmen gathered round him and muttered for a while. Then they produced one of the long poles and two lengths of grass rope. Lucius stepped in front of Marcus and refused to allow the tribesmen near him. He held out his arms and then pointed to the collapsed figure, indicating that he was prepared to carry him, and after another short consultation the tribesmen stepped aside in agreement.

Marcus's face was flushed and beaded with perspiration, and Lucius frowned in concern. He had seen these symptoms before and knew what they meant. Once there had been a girl. It seemed a long time ago now, but her memory was very fresh and Lucius knew that what happened to her would happen again . . . By evening Marcus would be raving and by the following morning he would be dead. But Lucius could not leave him here. He heaved the inert form into his arms and set off.

Marcus struggled and tried to escape, but the movement was weak and Lucius spoke soothingly to him and eventually he was quiet except for an occasional mutter which Lucius could not understand.

But the weather, which had dogged them from the start, was against them again. Perversely, today the sun decided to shine from a cloudless blue sky, and as the previous day's dampness was drawn from the ground it became unbearably humid and airless under the trees, and soon Lucius found himself gasping for breath.

Stops became more frequent to allow him to rest, though the tribesmen became increasingly impatient and once produced the carrying pole again. But Lucius was past caring about what happened to him now. All he knew was that he would not allow either Marcus or himself to undergo the agony of being transported in that way any more. He seized the pole, snapped it across his knee and flung the two pieces at the feet of the tribesman who had been holding it.

For a moment he thought he had gone too far. There was an angry murmur and he could see the red light of fury blazing in their eyes. Then one of them said something in their own language and they calmed themselves with difficulty.

Once again it was clear that he and Marcus were being saved for something special.

By mid afternoon Lucius noticed through the trees ahead the curious conical shapes of three almost identical hills. Had Marcus been in a fit state he could have told him that this was Trimontium, with the old

Roman signal station on the top of the nearest hill and the fort some distance to the north east.

But he was not really interested. His eyes were almost blinded with sweat, and it was as much as he could do to shamble forward in the wake of the three tribesmen in front. Marcus had become a dead weight in his arms and he was near the end of his strength.

He was scarcely aware of a new group of skin-clad tribesmen joining them, but he felt the jabs of their fingers and spear shafts in the tender parts of his body and he shook his head like a tired and baffled bear when the dogs had been baiting it for too long.

Painted arms relieved him of his burden and he mumbled a protest but no one understood the language he used. He stood swaying in a clearing in the forest as his spinning head slowed and the sweat cleared from his eyes.

And then he saw the fish.

At first he thought he had become delirious like Marcus, but as he blinked and stared at the strange object he knew that it was real—a huge silver fish, almost as high as the surrounding trees, standing upright on its fins, the sunlight glinting off its surface. The charred and blackened clearing round the fish was filled with tribesmen, and as he looked at them he saw them suddenly sink to their knees, facing the trees in the opposite direction from which he had come. A kind of strangled gasp came from them. Lucius turned and felt himself gasp too as from the shelter of the trees stepped the giant figure of the god.

5

The journey remained mercifully hazy to Marcus. He had blurred memories of being jolted and bumped in Lucius's arms and of the swaying branches of the trees patterning the blue sky beyond, and later he had an impression that someone was murmuring gently in the tribesmen's language in an accent which was not that of a tribesman, while some kind of soothing ointment was rubbed into his wrists and ankles and he was forced to drink a sharp, bitter-tasting liquid which brought a welcoming blackness.

After that there was nothing until he suddenly opened his eyes and stared round him in wonder, his head clear, and when he looked at his wrists and ankles he saw that already there was healthy scar tissue forming and that the deadly suppuration had disappeared.

His eyes took in a wider radius and he frowned in puzzlement. He was lying on some kind of soft couch, and in front of his eyes was a flat surface facing downwards towards him. On this surface were small circles with figures round the edge, though what the figures represented he had no means of knowing. There were rows of buttons and projections whose purpose he could not even begin to guess at.

There was an alienness about his surroundings which should have frightened him, but at the moment he seemed not to care and to be wrapped in a comforting cocoon of contentment.

"How do you feel?" a voice asked in the language of the tribesmen, but which was heavily overlaid with the accent he had heard in his delirium.

"I feel good," he said, and he turned.

He was lying in some kind of hut which seemed to be high above the ground, for when he looked out of the door beside him the ground was a long way below. But he could only see a little of the ground because most of the doorway was filled by the head and shoulders of a man. That was all Marcus could see, but by the width of the shoulders and the size of the head he knew that the man was enormous. He seemed young, with a smooth, beardless face and deep wrinkles round the eyes and the mouth, and a shock of golden-colored hair. The face was as strange as his surroundings, but it looked kind and he was not concerned.

"I am glad," said the face. "You will feel a little sleepy, but that is the effect of the drugs I have given you. Your wrists and ankles will be better by tomorrow."

Marcus nodded as if this was the most natural thing in the world.

"You are the god," he said.

The stranger smiled a little wryly.

"That would seem to be so," he said. "You are a—Roman, as these people talk of?"

"We are both Roman citizens," said Marcus. "But we do not come from Rome. Lucius's great-grandfather was a Roman legionary from Gaul. Mine was of the Brigantes, the tribe which lives just south of the Wall."

A line of worry appeared on the god's face.

"Where are the Romans?" he asked.

"The true Romans have almost all gone. There is trouble with warring tribes near the heartland of the Empire.

"But you—you are skilled in Roman ways since you are a Roman citizen?"

There seemed to be a throbbing anxiety in the god's voice, and Marcus shrugged.

"I have some skills. Lucius has others. Why do you ask?"

"What do you know about metal?"

"Metal? Very little. You mean iron? Lead? Gold? All these can be found in this country, I know."

The god shook his head impatiently.

"No, that is no good," he said. "I need—" and he said a word which sounded like *corenium*, though Marcus could not be sure. Whatever it was it meant nothing to him.

"I have never heard of such a metal," he said, and

38

even in his oddly disembodied state he felt troubled at the look of despair which crossed the god's face.

"You are sure? Do you know if any of your people would know?"

"It may be that some of them have knowledge of such a thing, but I certainly have none myself."

"Your friend? Might he know?"

"I shouldn't think so. Why don't you ask him?"

"I do not yet understand your language and he does not speak the tongue of these people." The god's face seemed to twist with pain and he turned away. "Rest quietly," he said. "You and your friend and I will speak again soon. There is much for me to think about."

His head and shoulders disappeared from the opening, and a moment later Marcus saw him stride across the clearing to the shelter of the trees, his head bent and his hands clasped behind his back. The tribesmen backed away from him respectfully, but he seemed not to notice them. He was almost twice their height and Marcus knew that his first impression of the god's size had been right. But for all that, and in spite of the soothing effect of the drug, Marcus could sense his inner despair.

6

There is much information we must exchange," said the god. "My name is Trist."

They were sitting at the base of the huge silver fish in which Marcus had awakened that morning. Now the sun was setting behind the three hills to the west and a gentle breeze was stirring the branches of the trees at the fringe of the clearing and sending pieces of charred grass skeltering across the ground. At the far corner of the clearing a group of tribesmen squatted, watching their god and his sacrifice. There were no women or children amongst them. Watching over the god was men's business. Marcus was feeling in excellent spirits now. The effect of the drug had worn off, taking the remainder of the fever with it and leaving his head clearer than it had been since they started this venture. The god sat on the turf, his bulky-looking white suit with the open rounded neck glistening in the background light of the tribesmen's fires, and his golden hair glowing almost red.

"What I have to say may seem strange to you, but I assure you that it is the truth as far as I know it. A lot you may not understand. I came from the skies."

Marcus translated this for Lucius's benefit, and the big man glanced up between the branches of the trees at the fleecy white clouds sailing serenely past against the pale blue of the evening sky.

"You *are* a god," he said, his voice hoarse with wonder.

Trist smiled gently.

"I'm afraid not," he said. "I wish I were. Certainly these men around us think I am and will not believe otherwise no matter what I say."

"But you came from the sky. If you came from the sky you must be a god. Only gods can fly," said Lucius logically.

"Yes. In your world only gods can fly," said Trist sadly. "It is different in mine. Besides, gods do not die, do they? We do. One of us did. I buried my companion over there."

He gestured to a patch of ground which they could see had been recently turned over. Marcus guessed from the length of the grave that the stranger's companion must have been of the same giant size.

"Why did you come?" he asked.

"I did not wish to. It was an emergency. The ship was damaged. Now I wish to get away again, back to my own world and my own people. But without certain materials I can't do it. The damage to the ship must be repaired with a metal we call corenium. That is the first thing. Then I must find fuel . . ."

Marcus held up his hand in confusion. The stranger was introducing so many new concepts that it was hard enough to take in without the added burden of trying to translate for Lucius.

"When I landed, these people—the tribesmen, you call them—found me and took me for a god. They have treated me with great respect, and after some time I managed to learn enough of their language to converse with them. I knew straightaway that they were not sufficiently advanced in civilisation to help me, but they spoke of a people to the south of here who were skilled in many arts, and I asked if it would be possible to meet any of them. Four days later they brought you."

Marcus nodded. This he could follow, and now the tribesmen's desire to preserve their health and strength was explained. They were to be sacrificed to their new god, as he had thought. And that realization brought a further piece of enlightenment.

"How long is it since your ship crashed?" he asked.

Trist smiled a little tiredly.

"Too long," he said. "It is thirty of your days and nights. I have sent endless messages of distress but no one answers my call . . . I'm sorry. There are no words in this language to describe how I do that. None of my people has come to help me. I seem to be alone . . ."

He relapsed into silence as Marcus, rather uncomfortably, translated what he had said for the benefit of Lucius. So this was why the tribes had banded together in the first place, this was the common bond which would give them the numbers and the strength to attack the Wall successfully. He and Lucius had discovered what they had come to discover. All that remained was where would the attack take place . . . ?

Trist's pale blue eyes seemed to be focused on some

41

far horizon beyond the trees and hills of this bleak land. Marcus was silent, partly because he was uncomfortable in the sad withdrawal of the giant who, despite his size, seemed curiously vulnerable, but also because so much of what the stranger had said gave rise to so many other questions. He could accept that the stranger had come from a world beyond the skies. Did not men say that the new god Jesus, who was growing so popular, lived in another world somewhere up there? But how could the stranger send messages to them? And how could this silver fish fly when it was so clearly heavier than air?

Marcus felt it would be better not to pursue these thoughts. They simply set his mind reeling again, so he coughed and began to explain his side of things, the background to life on either side of the Wall, the differences between the tribesmen in the north and the civilization in the south which the Wall sharply divided, the fact that as a trader he knew these tribesmen as well as any Roman Briton south of the Wall, and that it had been obvious to him from his last expedition to trade that the tribes had found something which had brought them together and united them.

"I think that something was you," he said.

"This is true," said Trist, nodding his golden head in the fading light. "They keep bringing more tribesmen to—worship me, I suppose. To begin with I tried to stop it, but it puzzled them and, I think, angered them, it seemed better to allow them to continue."

"Have they ever mentioned attacking the Wall?"

"No. Though I know they have no love for your people. I think they do not understand you."

Marcus nodded.

"As we do not altogether understand them. We think they are massing for an attack on us. It has happened many times before. With you as their new god they believe they will succeed. And now we are weaker. Our

42

strongest troops have left us and we are alone to defend the Wall as best we can. Unless we know where they attack they may conquer us."

Trist was silent, staring thoughtfully at the ground, tracing a pattern in the charred turf with a huge forefinger. At last he looked up.

"These Romans you spoke of. They are skilled metalworkers?"

"Oh, yes. They are very clever at most things."

"But there are no longer any of them where you come from?"

"South of the Wall there are still some Roman craftsmen like metalworkers."

Trist nodded, but Marcus had the feeling that he was not altogether convinced.

"I would like to meet one of these metalworkers," he said suddenly. "I wonder if this can be arranged? Even if he does not know of corenium he might be able to do something under my directions if we can find the raw materials. Or maybe find a substitute . . . The only thing is, I dare not leave the ship. The tribesmen might damage it if I am not here, and it is already badly damaged. Would it be possible for you to bring a metal worker here?"

Marcus frowned doubtfully.

"I could find a man easily enough, but whether he would be willing to risk his life coming north of the Wall is another matter."

"I could pay him—and you—with things whose value you could not estimate. I can give you a machine which would enable you to know in advance where the tribesmen are going to attack. I could even give you machines which would let you talk to a man many hundreds of miles away. However, wait one moment, and I will show you something of what I can do."

He rose to his feet, towering above them, and strode to the ladder clipped against the side of the ship and

43

began to climb it. There was a stir amongst the tribesmen as they shifted position to watch his movements, and then the small, dark faces turned almost with one accord and stared speculatively at them. The thought behind the intense eyes was so clear it might have been spoken. When was the god going to kill the sacrifices? Marcus shivered.

Trist reappeared from the silver fish and came down the ladder again, every movement followed and studied with anticipation by the tribesmen. In his hand he held a small white oval object about the size of a spearhead.

He sat down beside them again.

"Listen, and don't be frightened," he said. One of his fingers moved and there was a slight click from the white thing in his hand. "My name is Trist," he said, holding it fairly close to his mouth. "I have come from the skies from another world and I need your help. The bearer of this message will explain anything you wish to know and translate it into your own language, but I am giving you this machine as an example of the powers I can give you if you will help me in return."

He went on to give details of the metalworker he needed and then there was some complicated talk involving figures which Marcus could not understand. He wondered, too, why Trist was bothering to tell them these things all over again.

After some time Trist finished, and Marcus caught the flick of his finger again and heard the click repeated. Then Trist held up the small white thing and his finger moved once more. Again came the click and immediately the machine spoke.

"My name is Trist," it said. *"I have come from the skies from another world and I need your help . . ."*

Marcus felt his heart turn cold and out of the corner of his eye he saw that Lucius's face had gone deadly pale. This was magic indeed! The machine was saying exactly what Trist had said and it was using Trist's

44

voice! So far as he could remember every word, every inflection, was identical, although the volume of sound coming from the machine was lower than Trist had used, possibly because the machine did not want the tribesmen to hear it. Marcus gazed at the white machine in awe.

After a few moments Trist's finger moved again and the voice obediently stopped.

"Tonight," said Trist himself, "you will return to your people and take this machine with you. Give it to your Legate and press this button here. Each time you do that you will hear my voice. It is a message to your Legate and I hope when he hears it he may help you to help me."

"We—take the machine?" Marcus murmured uneasily.

"Yes. Do not be afraid. The machine is absolutely harmless. I give you my word. In a minute I shall take you to the cabin of my ship again and from there you will be able to escape."

Marcus glanced at the shadowy forms of the tribesmen some distance away.

"How?" he asked. "They will see us."

"No. I have thought of that," said Trist. "As soon as it is completely dark we shall move. That will give you most of the night to get well away from here."

Trist held out the machine and Marcus hesitantly took it from him. It was smooth and light in weight and fitted snugly into the shape of his hand.

"Press that button," said Trist.

Marcus felt around the smooth surface of the machine and found a small projection. He pressed it gently.

"My name is Trist," said the machine softly. *"I have come from the skies . . ."*

It was almost a reflex action to press the button again and stop the voice. Marcus felt his head spinning.

45

How could Trist's voice come from the machine when Trist himself was standing some distance away? And how was it that he, Marcus, could start and stop Trist's voice whenever he wanted to? These were questions he could not begin to answer.

"All right," he said a little shakily. "We will do our best."

7

Remembering how the tribes had boldly used the old road when they had been brought to Trimontium, Marcus and Lucius kept off it, but stayed close to it in the forest as they made their way southwards.

Marcus found it hard to believe that they were on their way back. There was so much to think of, so many inexplicable events which had occurred within the past day, that it would take him weeks of careful thought to marshal everything that he had learnt or been shown. His hand curled protectingly round the white machine.

Trist had escorted them up the ladder to the cabin of the fish as twilight was deepening into night. Behind them the dim figures of the watching tribesmen had seen them go. Lucius and Marcus had entered the ship and sat on the couches inside. There was not enough room for Trist to enter as well, so he stayed outside, his huge body blocking the view of the inside of the cabin from the watchers on the ground. And then in a low voice he had explained to them exactly what they must do.

When he had finished he looked at them for a while, and in the dim glow of the cabin light, whose source Marcus could not discover, they could see that his face was sad.

"Thank you for what you are doing," he said. "I

wish you well and I hope we shall meet again before too long. Farewell."

He held out an enormous hand and they took it in turn. Then Trist had slammed the cabin door shut and through the window they had seen him climb down the ladder and stride away into the trees. Many of the attendant tribesmen followed at a respectful distance.

They waited for a few minutes and then the view through the windows began to get cloudy. It was as if a fog grew thicker and thicker until the transparent, impenetrable openings through which they had been able to see into the outside world had become as solid as the walls of the cabin itself.

Immediately Lucius grunted and knelt up on his couch. He pulled forward the back of the seat and there behind it was a big, jagged gap torn in the floor of the cabin.

Lucius eased himself into the hole very gently and found that it was wide enough for him to get through. He nodded in satisfaction. Marcus saw him disappear through the opening and a faint scuffling noise echoed up to him.

From what Trist had said this hole had been partly responsible for the accident to the fish, but Marcus was not quite sure exactly how it had happened. However, this was Trist's instruction, and he lowered himself through the hole. For a moment his feet felt nothing but air as he hung from the tubular supports of the couch above, and then he felt Lucius's hand seize his ankle and guide it to a foothold.

A metal ladder was fixed to the wall of the ship and he lowered himself down it. There was light down there too, and he could make out strange dim shapes, pipes, tubes, huge metal boxes, all glowing in the hidden lighting and looking terribly menacing and alien. He was glad he could hear the muttered curses of Lucius just below him. It was something familiar.

47

As they reached the bottom of the ladder the shadows grew deeper. The light did not seem to penetrate as far as this, but just to the right of the ladder Marcus saw a patch of greyer darkness. It was suddenly blotted out as Lucius pushed his way through, and Marcus quickly followed. They stood outside the fish, between two of its tail fins, hidden from the watching tribesmen by the bulk of the fish itself, and behind them the covering of the trees was only a couple of paces away.

"The holes will be your escape route," Trist had said, "but those holes must be repaired with corenium before I can leave again."

They had soon put two or three miles between them and the silver fish, and there had been no sudden outcry to show that their escape had been discovered.

A little later the moon rose in the clear frosty sky above the trees and bathed them in a ghostly pale light.

Another mile or so, thought Marcus, and then they would rest. It might be best for the remainder of their night's trip if they moved away from the road. If their absence was discovered, that was where the tribesmen would search first. He told Lucius what he intended and the big man grunted and nodded. Marcus plunged through the undergrowth away from the road, heading deeper into the forest.

It was impossible to move quietly here and Marcus, clutching the white machine in one hand, was nervously aware of the crash of breaking branches and the rustle of knee-high grass as he and Lucius forced back the barriers to their progress.

They reached a clearing in the trees and after a quick pause to make sure there was no one in view Marcus led the way across it. The ground was bare here and the sudden cessation of noise made the night seem unusually still.

There was a sudden muffled thump and he heard

48

Lucius grunt. He glanced round involuntarily. The big man was no longer following him. Marcus stopped and turned and felt his heart lurch when he saw Lucius lying on the ground in the moonlight. He went back and knelt beside the still form, and it was only then that he saw the shaft of the arrow with its goose quill flights still thrumming slightly between Lucius's shoulder blades.

Marcus felt himself go suddenly cold. His immediate instinct was to take to his heels and run, put as much distance between himself and the clearing as he could before his strength gave out. But he stayed where he was and turned Lucius gently over on to his side. He was still breathing, but in shallow gasps as though each one was agony, and a thin dribble of blood, black in the moonlight, ran down the side of his mouth. Marcus put down the white machine beside him the better to cradle Lucius's head in his arms. The big man stared up at him with a puzzled look on his face, and his mouth moved. Marcus bent his head to hear what he wanted to say, but all that came out was a tired grunt, pathetically like the grunt which was so much a part of his normal conversation. Then the mouth went slack and the eyes seemed to glaze over in the moon light and the big body went limp.

For a few moments Marcus knelt there, with Lucius's head cradled in his arms, numb with shock and grief, and then he pulled himself together. He gently laid Lucius back on the ground and reached out a hand for the white machine.

A bare foot stamped down on his wrist, catching it at a bad angle. He heard a dry snap, his hand went numb, and then the pain seared up his arms as he was seized by the hair and dragged to his feet.

Through tears of pain he saw a group of tribesmen in front of him, faces painted in hideous designs, lank hair matted with pig fat, each carrying a spear and a sword with a shield slung across his shoulders.

This was not a hunting party. This was a war band.

One of them, a grizzled-looking veteran with an empty eye socket and wearing an iron helmet, seemed to be the leader. He stepped forward as Marcus cradled his broken wrist in his other hand.

"Spies," he said gutturally. "Roman spies."

And he spat in Marcus's face.

Marcus raised his good hand to wipe his face, but it was seized roughly from behind and his arm was forced behind and up until he thought it was going to break. He found himself arched over backwards like a taut bow.

Another tribesman seized his other hand to force it round as well, and Marcus screamed in agony.

He must have fainted, though not for long, because when the red mists of pain cleared from his eyes the tribesmen seemed to be standing in the same place and the moon was still shining serenely down from the same quarter of the sky.

But the leader had the white machine in his hand and was examining it curiously with his one eye. Other tribesmen were leaning over to see the strange thing, muttering to each other. Suddenly the leader held it out.

"What is this?" he asked.

Marcus shook his head. He had no idea what it was in any case, but he had no chance to reply, for the leader must accidentally have touched the button, and immediately the voice spoke clearly.

"My name is Trist," it said. *"I have come from the skies . . ."*

In his astonishment the leader dropped the white machine. The voice broke off abruptly as it hit the ground, and the tribesmen stared at each other, eyes wide and blazing in their painted faces.

"The voice of the god," muttered the leader. "He has stolen the voice of the god!"

"He has killed the god!" said another.

50

The voices growled like a threatening thunder. The noise grew louder and in the mists of pain Marcus saw them drawing nearer, the painted faces mouthing obscenely, the eyes seeming to glow with a hellish fanatical light of their own, their fetid breath making him retch. He tried to get away, but he was firmly pinned and his movement only increased the pressure on his arms.

The pain flowed over him again and darkness welled around him.

He had already lost consciousness when the spear was driven into his chest.

8

Trist sat in the open cabin doorway as he had sat for more days than he cared to think of. He had patched and tidied and repaired everything in the scout ship that he could, but there was nothing more he could do until the two Romans returned with help.

He sighed, his chin cupped in his hand, and gazed distastefully down at the clearing below him and the patch of earth where Greet lay. Already the grass was beginning to cover it and soon it would be unrecognizable. It was a lonely business being a god.

His last hope was in the Romans, and deep within himself he knew that it was an extremely forlorn one. The two men the tribesmen had brought to him were certainly far more advanced than the Picts, but from what they had said their culture had been stronger some time before and seemed now to be retrogressing. Even at its height he found it difficult to believe these people could produce metal like corenium. The Romans' reaction to the standard of technology in the ship was enough to make that clear, and the mutual language of the savage tribesmen had been totally inadequate for explanations on the recorder. He wished he had had

51

more time with the Romans to learn their language, which seemed to offer so much more scope, but although he had recordings of everything they had said, including Marcus's translations, he had had no time to study them.

He was stupid to hope for anything from this venture, but if there was no hope in this there was no hope in anything.

A stir in the camp below jerked his mind away from these gloomy thoughts. A group of tribesmen appeared from the fringe of trees and approached the ship. When they were within twenty paces of it they stopped and knelt down.

Trist sighed. This was the usual signal that they wanted to consult him about something, so he climbed down the ladder to the ground, raised a hand and said, "I greet you."

The leader looked at him out of his one eye.

"It is good to see the mighty Trist," he said. "We thought he had deserted us."

"Why should you think that?" asked Trist.

"Our battle went ill," said the leader. "The Roman Wall is stronger than we thought. We lost many warriors. They lost many too, but not enough, and we thought Trist had deserted us. I see the fault is ours. The thought sapped our manhood. We lack faith. But what else were we to think when we heard the voice of Trist in the hands of the Romans?"

Trist stood quite still.

"What do you mean?" he asked, although already he had a horrible idea that he knew the answer.

The leader turned to the fringe of the wood and gestured. Four tribesmen appeared carrying between them two limp forms which they dropped on the ground at Trist's feet.

"Roman spies had stolen Trist's voice," said the leader. "This we did not understand. But we have brought Trist's voice back to him. It is a great miracle and a sign of Trist's power that he still has a voice and yet it is also contained in this box. We carried the Roman spies and the box on our attack, but it did not prosper."

And he held out the white machine.

Trist's roar of rage brought the other tribesmen to their feet and sent his birds fluttering in panic from the surrounding trees. The leader fell back a step, not understanding, but Trist reached out a huge hand, gripped the man by the throat, lifted him bodily into the air and flung him with immense force into the trunk of the nearest tree.

There was a moan of terror and amazement from the tribesmen as they heard a sound as though a branch of the tree had snapped, although there was no branch as low on the trunk, and the body of the leader slithered to the ground and lay twitching, twisted at an odd angle. They had never seen the god angry before.

They watched in awe as the huge figure turned his face to the sky in a look of appeal, and were astonished to see tears falling from his eyes. Then he turned and staggered to the ladder which led to his shrine, climbed up it and disappeared inside. The door slammed shut and they were left wondering what they ought to do to appease him and when he would return to them.

But he never did. The silver fish remained silent and the name of Trist became nothing more than a fading legend to the painted people.

INTERLUDE

Trist sat on his couch, forehead resting on the console, shivering uncontrollably. He should not have given way like that. It showed the danger of building hopes on weak foundations.

He had opaqued the viewports of the ship so that he could not see what was happening in the clearing below, but he knew the leader of the tribesmen was dead. The trouble was he found it difficult to judge his strength on this planet. Gravity was far less than it was on Haven and consequently movement was easier and his strength seemed greater.

His last link with a possible civilization had disappeared with the production of those two sad bundles. Tht men who, unlike the tribesmen, he could regard to some extent as people like himself, were dead. The worst thought of all was that he was largely responsible for their deaths. He had sent them back to their side of the Wall and they had been intercepted and killed. Possibly he could have saved them, but not knowing the workings of the tribesmen's minds he did not see what else he could have done.

In any case he had to face the facts now. The culture in this world was far too primitive to be of any use to him. Even the Roman culture at its greatest would have been nowhere near sufficient.

He himself had not the qualifications to find and refine corenium, even if the raw materials existed on this planet.

Therefore there was only one thing he could do.

He opened the locker in the center of the console and

took out the little transparent packet from the first aid box. Inside were two small blue capsules. Trist broke the seal round one of them and held it between the finger and thumb of one hand, looking at it.

There was nothing to stop him. He had no wish to face the tribesmen outside again. The radio was set permanently on the distress frequency and would faithfully beam out his message forever or until it was switched off, the batteries drawing power from the planet's primary. He could be asleep in a matter of minutes and his worries would be over.

When his distress call was eventually picked up he would be rescued. He found it difficult to understand why Captain Graud had so far failed to answer, but doubtless there were reasons why he had not done so. Trist was sure, however, that the captain would not abandon the search for him.

If for some reason he was not found he would know nothing about it. No one knew how long the sleep pill lasted. It might be forever, but at least it should be long enough to allow the culture on this planet to develop sufficiently to provide him . with corenium or an adequate substitute when he awoke.

He checked the cabin, and to preserve power for the radio, left on only the dim green glow of the console light. He checked that the radio was still sending out the recorded message and that everything else was switched off.

It was done.

He hesitated with the capsule half way to his mouth. Suddenly it seemed as though he was committing suicide, but the idea was ridiculous, he told himself. He was simply putting himself to sleep, suspending animation until such time as it would be worth resuming his life again.

He took a deep breath, put the capsule in his mouth and swallowed it.

Then he settled back on the couch and tried to relax, staring at the green light of the instruments on the console. It seemed as though a greyness was creeping into the edges of his vision, and he tried to blink it away. It refused to go, and crept in further. The green of the console contracted silently and swiftly into a pinpoint of light which seemed to glow brightly for a split second before going out.

TWO

1

Nicol Snaith curled the ends of his hair off his collar and looked at himself appreciatively in the mirror. He half-hooded his eyes and let the corners of his mouth droop in an expression of passion, and then stood back a little. The pimples weren't too bad today, and probably Prudence wouldn't notice them in the artificial light. By the time she was close enough to spot them it would be dark anyway, so that should be all right.

Prudence, he thought wryly. Oh, well. It wasn't exactly what you could describe as a conquest. Where most of the girls in the Social Security Sixth Typing Pool delighted in displaying themselves as much as possible to the male gaze, Prudence was the exact opposite. Which was hardly surprising. When most girls with bad sight wore contact lenses so no one would know, Prudence stuck to big tortoiseshell spectacles. When most girls emphasised their figures with almost non-existent skirts, spray-on stockings and jumpers which must have stopped them from breathing, Prudence wore long, shapeless dresses and old-fashioned tights. With her spaniel-like face, her spindly thighs and her quite inadequate breasts she was not everyone's idea of the perfect night out.

But she had one priceless asset as far as Nicol Snaith was concerned. Her uncle was Clerk to the Appointments Board, and on the assumption that the quickest way to a man's heart was through his only living relative, Nicol Snaith was prepared to undergo any form of mental or physical torture.

Briefly the thought flashed through his mind that, presented with Prudence naked and probably ashamed, he might not be able to manage it, but he pushed the thought scornfully aside. He was potent enough, he had no doubt of that.

He had worked a long time on this, tracing the relationships of those in high places who might prove useful, cultivating Prudence once he'd discovered who her uncle was. He wouldn't be sitting for much longer in that foul office at one of the two hundred and fifteen desks filling in endless P. 3649 forms. He had always known he was cut out for better things.

He picked up the box of cheap chocolates from the bed and, whistling cheerfully to himself, he left the room.

He would have to move fairly fast. There was an Appointments Board meeting next month, and in that time he had to work his way so effectively into Prudence's affections that she would introduce him to her uncle as her fiancé. He would be on his best behavior, of course, asking permission to marry the girl, hoping that Uncle would consider his prospects good enough for so wonderful a person as Prudence, and he'd drop a subtle hint or two that he would like to get into the Investigating Department. Then he would leave the rest to fate. He was quite sure that, presented with this situation a week or so before the Appointments Board met, Prudence's uncle would be prepared to push him.

Once he had the job all would be well. He could

57

drop Prudence and take up the search for someone a little more to his taste. After a month of Prudence it would be a relief to get his arms round a real woman with the right ideas and the right shape.

He left the Bachelor Apartment Block and set off along the street, bordered with exactly similar blocks, towards the massive Department of Employment and Productivity Building, permanently aglow with light from every one of its thousands of windows, towering twenty stories into the sky.

The Investigating Department, he thought, and licked his lips in anticipation. To be an Investigating Officer. To·have the power of one of those quiet, expressionless men. To be treated with respect and servility wherever you went. To be able to go to the front of the queue in the canteen and not be shouted at. To be allowed first into the lift when the crowds were waiting impatiently to get away at sixteen hundred hours. That was the life.

And there was another thing, too. Investigating Officers had first right of entry into the underground shelters when the alarm went . . .

If his plan worked he might well be one of the élite band before two months had passed.

Well, it started tonight. He looked up at the sky and sniffed the air. It was warm and settled, no wind, there would be a moon later, twilight was falling and the stage seemed set for romance.

Nicol Snaith whistled as he walked towards the Productivity Building, and already there was an unconscious swagger in his stride, the kind of swagger usually associated with the uniformed branch of the Investigating Department.

2

Prudence Briggs stood beside Number Seven Entry

of the Productivity Building, her hands clasped tightly in front of her. She was wearing an old tweed skirt which reached to within three inches of her knees and a brown cardigan which hung limply from her narrow shoulders.

"Don't bother to dress," Nicol had said with a meaningful look which had filled her with a dreadful anticipation.

She was not quite sure what she felt about Nicol Snaith. He did not come up to the expectations of her dreams, but she was realist enough to know that that was hardly likely anyway. He was smaller than her ideal, and there was something about him which she mistrusted, though she did not know what it was. He had been polite and thoughtful to her in a way which very few men ever were, and for this she was grateful. In the weeks since he had taken to visiting the Social Security Sixth Typing Pool and had begun to talk to her, to show an interest in what she had to say and to concern himself with her welfare she had experienced a feeling she had never known before. Although there were undercurrents of deeper emotions which scared her a little it was mainly compounded of gratitude. Gratitude for his concern and for enabling her to feel that after all she was a woman and someone cared about her, however slightly.

Tonight was the first time he had asked her out. For days she had wondered if he would and had almost despaired of him ever doing so, and when he eventually did she said yes so quickly and with such heartfelt enthusiasm that she had felt ashamed.

Through the glass doors of the entry she could see the hall clock pointing at nineteen hundred hours exactly, and she felt her heart speed up with delicious discomfort. This was the time.

She wondered if Uncle Victor would approve. She had said nothing to him, but had felt no pang of conscience at her omission. She had scarcely seen him for weeks. He was a very busy man, constantly worried by the onerous responsibilities of his work. He treated her with a correct and distant affection which was totally inadequate in many ways, and although she kept house for him in his Class II Executive Standard Dwelling, their paths rarely crossed. Uncle Victor was out most evenings, dining with important visiting Ministry and Department representatives, and she generally had the house to herself, keeping loneliness at bay by immersing herself in re-reading the classics which had been her companions for so long and to such little purpose at school and at university.

Now tonight there was growing before her something more interesting and exciting than Horace's Odes or Caesar's Gallic Wars, and she found herself quivering with anticipation of something she did not fully understand.

He was five minutes late, and she had begun to wonder if after all, she had imagined everything, that he had never asked her out for the evening, and the high beat of her heart had slowed to a dull throb of defeat, when she saw him appear round a corner of the building, his thick, dark hair falling to his shoulders, his sky-blue suit glowing in the lights from the windows. It was all she could do to stay where she was and wait calmly for him to reach her, when every instinct cried to her to run to him and cling to him and make sure he did not leave her.

"Hi, doll," he said, his teeth flashing in a brilliant smile.

"Hello, Nicky," she said a little breathlessly, and felt her face flaming. It was almost dark now and she hoped her change of color was not noticeable to him.

"Have a choc," he said and held out the box.

"Oh, Nicky, you shouldn't have."

" 'Course I should. Sweets to the sweet, as someone said."

She took the box and stood wondering what the next move should be. Any of the other girls in the office would know exactly what to do and say, but he seemed unaware of her uncertainty.

"Come on, doll. You and me are going for a walk. Okay?"

Without giving her a chance to reply he linked his arm through hers and began to lead her away from Number Seven Entry.

The touch of his arm seemed to melt her into helplessness and she felt her throat contract. She was unaware of where they were going. All she knew was that he was beside her, that his arm was warm through hers, that here at last was a man who cared. Later, when they had left the Town Complex behind and the moon was appearing over the three pronged rim of the hills ahead of them and he loosed his arm and put it round her waist, she felt tears rising in her eyes so that the view of the hills seemed to shimmer and dance in a joyful pattern reflecting her own happiness.

He turned aside from the road and helped her over a gate into a field, his hands strong round her waist as he lifted her down, and for a moment she stood on the far side, her head leaning against his chest, too happy to move.

The field sloped gently upwards towards a fringe of trees before the real rise to the hills began, and by the time they had reached the trees the stars were winking down from a clear, jet-black sky and the moon was hanging just over the tips of the hills. It was beautiful and almost full, and in this situation she found it impossible to believe that there was any danger lurking on that bright surface.

A fallen tree trunk blocked their path and Nicol stopped.

"Let's sit here, okay?" he said.

She sat down obediently on the mossy trunk, laying the box of chocolates beside her. He offered her a cigarette which she refused. He lit one himself and sat down beside her and put his arm round her waist again.

"You're a good doll," he said. "I like you. Y'know?"

She nodded shyly, but the tree trunk was in shadow and he could not see the movement.

"You know that, don't you, doll?" he persisted.

"I—I think so, Nicky," she said, hoping her voice sounded less quavery than it felt.

"No 'think' about it. It's true."

"I—I don't know why. I'm not pretty, and—and I can't say clever things—"

"You know what they say. Beauty's only skin deep. Reckon that's a fact. The things I feel for you, doll, they're more important than a pretty face. Or clever remarks. Heck, I'm not much good at expressing myself, don't have the knack of it. But you know what I mean."

His hand moved at her waist, and she felt his fingers gently unzipping her skirt. Then there was pressure from his hand and she found herself leaning against him. His other hand found her face and turned it towards him. For a moment she wanted to cough from the smoke of his cigarette, and then his mouth was on hers.

Since her parents had died in an air crash fifteen years before, a chilly peck on the cheek from Uncle Victor on her birthday and at Christmas was the only physical contact she had known. The touch of Nicky's mouth seemed to cause an explosion inside her. She responded eagerly and clumsily and as she turned to press herself to him her loosened skirt fell unheeded to her ankles. His right hand came up under her cardigan, exploring the corrugation of her ribs, and she quivered uncontrollably as it unhooked her brassière. Then his hand was on the flatness of her breast, and the sky and the moon and the stars seemed to swing round in a kaleidoscope of heavenly colours.

Then that marvellous exploring hand began to explore further and a little later her pants and tights were being eased down over her thin buttocks, and she was gasping and moaning in a way she would never have thought possible an hour before, her mouth hot and loose on his.

She felt him jerk slightly and saw him throw away his cigarette. For a split second she wondered how, if he was feeling the same way as she was, he could have held on to it for so long. But the thought passed in a tidal wave of ecstasy.

Her skirt, pants and tights were tangled round her ankles in an unwieldy mess and she kicked out of them. The warm, free night air on her legs and thighs seemed to add to her desire.

His hand came back to the edge of her cardigan and as it did so he broke away from her.

"Take it off, doll," he whispered, and began to pull the cardigan upwards.

Willingly she raised her arms and the cardigan and her loosened brassière slipped over her head. He flung them to the ground and she adjusted her glasses with an almost guilty gesture. She sat on the tree trunk, her body glowing white in the moonlight, thin and unshaped, trembling but oddly proud.

Nicol's hand stroked her flanks and she closed her eyes and moaned in an agony of rapture. Then suddenly there was an oath and his hands were gone.

She opened her eyes in shock and surprise. Nicol had risen from the tree trunk and was staring at something behind her right shoulder. She whirled round, hands automatically flying to cover herself. At the edge of the clearing stood a huge figure in a bulky white garment, and the moonlight glowed yellow on his hair.

"*Salvete,*" said the figure. "*Potestisne me adiuvare?*"

Damn him, thought Nicol Snaith. Things had been going so well, and then *he* had to appear out of nowhere!

Cheeks burning at the indignity of being discovered, he stood indecisively, wondering whether to give the intruder a piece of his mind or whether to get out fast.

A quick assessment of the stranger's size and probable strength convinced him that the latter course would be safer. He had no wish to face a fight in front of Prudence where it was obvious he would come off second best.

Prudence was crouching on the ground, frantically trying to gather her clothes together and keep herself hidden from the stranger at the same time when he grabbed her hand.

"Come on. Let's get out of here," he said viciously.

"Oh, Nicky—! Wait! I can't find—! Oh, Nicky, my clothes—!"

"Oh, shut up and let's go!" he snapped.

She had a handful of clothing in her other hand and he pulled her away. A last glance showed the stranger still standing in the shadows looking at them with a blank expression on his face. Stupid, interfering bastard!

He dragged Prudence through the trees, ignoring the sounds of her weeping. She cried out once as she stubbed her bare toe on a root, and at last tried to pull back.

"Nicky—please!" she panted. "I can't—I must get dressed! Nicky, stop, please!"

"Oh, all right!" he said, and he stopped just at the fringe of the trees and turned to her. She was clasping the bundle of clothes inadequately to her, her hair unkempt where branches had raked through it, her eyes puffy behind the glasses. She really looked pathetic, he thought. You'd hardly even realize she was a woman. He felt himself shivering with reaction and took a deep breath. Careful, he thought. It might be all right yet. Just a temporary setback.

"Okay. Get dressed, doll," he said, keeping his voice calm with an effort.

She stood quite still, her head lowered.

"Please, Nicky. Don't look," she said instinctively.

Moodily he turned away and stared out across the field towards the Town Complex. Don't look! Scraggy bitch, what was there to look at?

He heard muffled sobs begin again after a moment and he fought down his irritation and turned back. She had put on the shapeless cardigan and was zipping up her skirt, her tights in one hand.

"What's the matter?" he asked, controlling his voice with an effort.

"I—I've only got my skirt and my cardigan and one shoe," she said forlornly. "I haven't got my—anything else."

"Well, we can't go back for them. You should have made sure."

"You didn't give me a chance," she said with more defiance than he had ever heard from her.

"Look doll, forget about them," he said placatingly, putting his hands on her shoulders. "Tell you what. Tomorrow I'll buy you some new things. How about that, eh? Know just the place. I'll buy you things'll make you feel like a new woman."

"I don't know—"

"Honest I will. You'll look real good, doll, I'm telling you."

"Well—"

"That's my baby. You got enough to be going on with. Okay now?"

He spoke gently and insistently to her, but for some reason she refused to meet his eye. Probably ashamed or something.

"I must look a mess," she sniffed.

Nothing unusual in that, he thought.

"Not you. You look great, doll. Honest, you do. Come on. I'll see you home."

He took her hand and squeezed it but there was no answering pressure and she still refused to meet his eye. He began to lead her back across the field towards the gate. She walked slowly, concentrating on where she was putting her feet, carrying her one remaining shoe, and he was conscious that a barrier which had never existed before had suddenly come between them.

Damn it, he thought. If that was so, he wasn't just back at square one. He was behind it. And the Appointments Board met in a month's time.

4

Uncle Victor was still out, and Prudence was surprised to see by the wall clock that it was only twenty one hundred hours. It seemed ages since she had met Nicky at Number Seven Entry.

She wanted to wash and do her hair, but somehow she could not bear the thought of looking at herself in a mirror, so she simply found another pair of shoes to put on and sat down in the living room, staring miserably at the curtained window.

The whole evening had been too awful to think about. She wondered if she would ever be able to look Nicky in the face again. The way he had dragged her away without giving her a chance to find all her clothes . . .

She stared at the wall in growing horror.

66

Her clothes!

The bra and pants she had worn had been a birthday present from Uncle Victor. At least, Uncle Victor had given her the money and she had used it to buy the underclothes and he had harrumphed and hastily changed the subject when she had told him what she had spent the money on. And they had her initials embroidered on them. They had been expensive and she had felt terribly extravagant. After all, why have underwear with your initials on? She was never likely to leave them where they would require identification. And now that very thing had happened. If anyone found them under the tree trunk, what would they think? The news could be round the Department Building in a flash!

But she couldn't go back. She might meet the stranger again.

It was funny that since it had happened she had hardly thought about the stranger. To her he had merely been a slightly shadowy figure she had noticed in the height of her emotional fever, but now the recollection of his presence did not fill her with distaste as she might have expected.

He had spoken. It had registered on her mind at the time that there was something odd about it. What was it? She squeezed her eyes shut in an effort to remember.

He hadn't spoken in English. What had he said? It was on the tip of her tongue. *Salvete.* That had been the first word, and she frowned in astonishment as she remembered it. And then she had the whole thing. *Potestisne me adiuvare?*

With quiet determination she slipped on her shoes and made her way out of the house.

The stranger had asked if they could help him. That was odd enough. But it was a great deal odder that he had asked them in Latin.

The moon was high when she reached the wood. On

67

that bright surface strangely suited men might be working on the rockets aimed menacingly at the planet below, but all that reached here now was the pure silver light, patchy pools of luminescence between the trees. She found her way back to the tree trunk, her heart beating a little faster than the exertion of getting here demanded.

There was no one here.

She felt an inexplicable pang of disappointment. The man had asked her for help. In all her life no one had ever done that before and an odd responsive warmth grew in her, an affection almost, which made her long to take the man and cradle his head in her lap . . .

She shook herself. It was difficult to understand the thoughts and feeling which had swept over her like successive waves of the sea during these last few days. But first things first. She approached the tree trunk, feeling a sense of shame at the abandonment which had seized her just an hour or so before. Really, she should have had more sense. Men never respected a woman who threw herself at them. She should have played him along, held him at arm's length in the way she so often heard the other girls in the Typing Pool say they had done.

Still, it was too late now. She crouched down and found her second shoe immediately. A little further searching produced her pants, then the box of chocolates, which she left, and then her brassière.

She stepped hastily into the pants and, after a quick glance round, pulled off her cardigan and slipped on the unnecessary brassière and then the cardigan on top of it.

There was still no sign of anyone nearby. A slight breeze rustled the branches over her head and the tracery of shadows on the ground shivered slightly.

"Hallo," she called softly, and immediately put a

hand to her mouth as though to try to force the word back.

Why had she done that? She shook her head. Alone in the wood, throwing herself at a second man in one night—something had really happened to her. Soberly she told herself this was dangerous. It was one thing coming here with Nicky, someone she knew and saw almost every day during working hours. It was quite another deliberately coming alone to the woods to seek out a stranger.

And yet somehow she felt more comfortable now than she had done with Nicky. She had only the vaguest recollection of what the stranger had looked like in those few hysterical moments before Nicky had dragged her away, but some deep instinct told her that there was no danger from him.

She began to walk deeper into the trees, holding her one extra shoe in her hand.

"Hello," she called again.

The wood was quite still. The undergrowth was becoming more dense now, and the long black fingers of the hawthorns pulled at the wool of her cardigan and the brambles tore at her bare legs. There would be scratches to explain in the Typing Pool tomorrow morning. "Here, Prudy, he must have been a right kinky one last night, eh?" they'd say, giggling and winking at each other, certain that she wouldn't have been anywhere near a man last night. Only she would have been. Very near one, and perhaps near another. If only she could tell them so. But they would only laugh disbelievingly and go on calling her Prudy which she hated.

"Hello," she called again, and the word was bitten off halfway as the bushes ahead of her parted and there he was.

The moon shone down through a gap in the trees

directly on to his face. She had not realised he was so big. Why, he must be over seven feet tall, and although it was difficult to tell in the strange bulky suit he wore, she was certain he was broad and muscular as well.

His face was open and gentle-looking and so far as she could tell in the deceptive moonlight his hair was pure gold. She wondered what color his eyes were, but they were deeply shadowed by the moon overhead.

He smiled at her, a gentle, tentative smile which seemed to fill her with a warmth she had never known with Nicky. She had heard the phrase somewhere about one's heart melting and had dismissed it as romantic claptrap. She would never do so again.

"*Salve*," he said, and there was a hesitance in his voice and a slight upward inflection as though he were not simply greeting her, but asking a question at the same time.

"*Salve*," she said, and his face lit into a delighted smile. "Why do you speak in Latin?"

When she spoke in English he looked blank and shook his head, and she realized he had not understood her. There were questions to be asked here, but that would come later. Hastily she summoned all her knowledge of Latin. It was very difficult to translate modern English into Latin, and she had to stop and think over the best way of rendering a question or a statement, so the conversation took a long time.

"Why do you speak in Latin?" she asked, using the language herself.

He hesitated for a moment.

"It had been a long time," he said. "It is the only language of yours I know. Except this one—"

And he suddenly switched to a strange, guttural tongue, full of throat-catching burrs and rattles, the like of which she had never heard before.

She shook her head in bewilderment.

"I do not understand that," she said. "Surely you must speak some other language."

"I do," he said. "But I know you will not understand *it*."

Again he switched tongues. This time it was a liquid, rather beautifully cadenced speech which sounded strangely as though it were compounded of many different languages. But it meant nothing to her.

"We must speak Latin," she said, and was surprised at the firmness in her voice.

"You do not normally speak Latin?" asked the stranger.

"I speak it a little. It's a dead language, though some people still study it. I like it."

"Then we shall use it, as you suggest," said the stranger and he held out his hand.

After a moment's hesitation she took it, feeling the huge palm and immensely strong fingers tighten gently round her hand, which seemed suddenly minute.

"There are many things you will not understand," he said quietly. "I want you to trust me."

She nodded immediately. She would trust him, she knew that deep down inside her. She had nothing to fear from him.

"I have come from a long way away," he said slowly and carefully, and she nodded, showing that she had understood the sentence. She began to realize that Latin was not as familiar to him as it had seemed at first. He had to search for words and sometimes his phrasing was clumsy. "And I need help. Do you know anything about metals?"

She shook her head, wishing there was a direct negative and affirmative in Latin.

"I know nothing of metals," she said.

"But men—they know about metals?"

"Men know."

71

"Have you ever heard of a metal called corenium?"

She shook her head again and he made a gesture of a sudden irritation.

"I am sorry," he said. "That name will mean nothing to you. It is in my language. How could you even know what the metal is? I have no means of giving you its basic elements."

"I would not understand it even if you could," she said.

He looked at her with an expression of extreme hopelessness on his face.

"What am I to do?" he muttered.

She felt her heart go out to him. He seemed to be so alone, isolated from everyone and everything in a way which she could understand so well, and she longed to be able to break down that isolation and to comfort him, knowing that if she could do so she would gain comfort herself. She laid her free hand on his.

"I could bring you books from the library," she said. "There are many books on metals. Perhaps you could find what you are looking for in them."

As hope grew in his face she broke off, for she had suddenly seen a barrier.

"But they will not be in Latin," she said.

"That does not matter," he said. "If you will spend a little time speaking your language I can copy it and feed it to my machine which will help me to understand it."

She felt the words he was using were inadequate because there were none more appropriate. But the most important thing was that he was asking her to spend some time with him, and she felt warmth spread through her. It was much the same warmth as she had felt when Nicky had asked her to go out with him for the first time, but there was a sense of security and happiness here, and a complete lack of doubt such as there had been with Nicky.

It was a night of magic. They sat on the mossy bank amongst the trees and he produced a strange white machine from a hidden pocket of his clothing and asked her to talk. She was hesitant at first, but gradually she gained in confidence as he listened assiduously to her talking in English, asking many questions in Latin to which she replied and translated, and as the moon swung downwards again in the west she found herself telling him of her dull life, of the work she did, the endless typing out of endless forms amongst hundreds of other people, a tiny cog in a vast machine which was gradually grinding to a halt under the weight of its own incompetence. She told him of her Uncle Victor, and of Nicky too, which showed how relaxed she had become. She even told him something of her secret dreams of marriage and of the large family she longed for, and a kind and considerate husband who perhaps might not be a civil servant in the Department of Employment and Productivity, but would be privileged to do important work in some more useful sphere. She surprised herself as she spoke, for many of the things she said she had not realized she felt before.

He was quiet most of the time and she was sure there must be much that he did not understand, but somehow that did not matter.

Many years before she had read *A Midsummer Night's Dream*, and the deep magic of that play seemed to re-echo here. This night too was timeless and divorced from reality. At the back of her mind she knew there were illogical elements, but she was content to ignore them for the time being. They were unimportant, and if they were resolved at a later date, well and good. If not it didn't matter at all.

It was only when she had left him as dawn was breaking and she was making her way over the field towards the road that the spell was finally broken, and

73

she looked up at the pale blue lightening sky with new eyes and a deeper peace inside her than she had known for many years. It suddenly came to her then that she knew nothing about the man. She did not even know his name. She had asked him none of the questions which had seemed important when she had set out to meet him. She did not know where he came from or why they had to speak Latin as their only mutual language, and which of the two others he had spoken was native to him.

Even with the spell broken and practical thoughts of Uncle Victor's breakfast and of the day's work in the Typing Pool crowding into her mind, these questions still remained ethereally in the background to be asked and answered only if the occasion should arise.

She slipped quietly into the house as the wall clock chimed six-thirty, had a bath, washed the bra and pants with the embroidered initials, called Uncle Victor and boiled his two medium eggs, listened with half an ear to his strictures over the latest outrage perpetrated by the Chinese Government, and left for the Typing Pool at the usual time.

The huge office seemed smaller and a lot shabbier than it had been the day before, and the girls around her more strident and shallow. She sat down at her desk, pressed her glasses firmly on to her nose, drew a pile of buff P. 3649 forms towards her and fed the first one into her machine.

Half an hour later a shadow fell across her desk. She looked up and found Nicky standing beside her, a sheaf of forms in his hands.

"Hi, doll," he said.

"Hello, Nicky."

He hesitated a moment.

"Here, I meant what I said, y'know," he said quickly and quietly, with a hasty glance round to make sure no

74

one was listening. "I mean about getting you new things."

"Oh, that's all right, Nicky," she said brightly. "You don't need to bother. I've got them back."

"Eh? You have?"

"Of course."

"How?"

"I went back for them."

His eyebrows rose in surprise.

"Here, doll, that must have taken some doing. Good for you."

Prudence smiled. Suddenly she realised that the voice which had given her so much pleasure sounded as false as hell. He didn't mean what he was saying. He never had done. The whole attempted seduction had been coldly planned—and she admitted frankly it would have succeeded if the stranger had not appeared. He had been playing with her for some reason which she couldn't fathom. Maybe to win a bet. Well, if that had been the case it was a bet he would never win, no matter how near he had come to it last night.

"See you tonight?" he said casually as he laid the forms down on her desk.

She looked up at him and smiled gently.

"I'm afraid not, Nicky," she said.

He froze and his eyes suddenly hardened.

"Oh? Why not?" he asked.

"Because I can't."

"What d'you mean, you can't? We agreed."

"I don't think I did," she said, feeling a sudden unaccustomed sense of power in her. For the first time in her life she had someone dangling on the end of the line. It was an experience as satisfying as it was unexpected.

"Aw, now, doll—"

"I can't, Nicky. I'm going out with someone else."

Her triumph evaporated and she flinched. For a moment she thought he was going to knock her down, there and then in the middle of the Typing Pool, but he didn't. His eyes had gone icy cold and his mouth was compressed into a thin, mean line. She wondered how she had ever thought of him as being attractive.

Then he turned and marched out, walking stiffly as though he were not quite certain of his legs.

5

It was a long corridor and his feet took him down it automatically. By the time he reached the door of his own office the white heat of fury had cooled to a disbelieving indignation.

She had given *him* the brush-off! In all his calculations and plans that was the one thing he had never taken into account because the possibility had seemed so remote as to be non-existent.

The bitch. Who the hell did she think she was? Animated sexless hairpin, how dare she?

He slammed into the office, causing the clerks at the nearer desks to look up from their work. He strode past the P. 4637 group, crossed through the P. 736 and SS. 19 areas to his own desk in the middle of the P. 3649 section.

Another pile of the endless buff forms had arrived on his desk during his absence and he stared at them unseeingly, pulled one towards him and began to copy on to a fresh form, with short, vicious strokes from his pen.

Name . . . Address . . . Age . . . National Insurance Number . . . National Service Number . . . Reasons for Application . . . Dependent Children . . . Dependent Relatives . . . When did you last receive National Assistance . . . ? Are you in receipt of any other Government grant or pension . . . ?

76

What had she meant, she was going out with someone else? That wasn't possible. Who on earth would want to go out with her? A girl friend, maybe. But he knew she had no girl friends. She never mixed with the other girls in the Typing Pool. That was one of the things which he had known would make his job easier. Her complete loneliness and isolation from human companionship.

Then who . . . ?

An idea came into his head just as the alarm bell clanged insistently and he laid down his pen and hurried towards the nearest emergency exit door with several dozen other clerks.

There was some talk and a little nervous laughter. These alarms had become so frequent recently that people were beginning to wonder if they were all just practice. Rumors flew round that they were not, that these were the real thing, but no one seemed to know for sure, and it formed a pleasant break to the day's dull routine.

Life would be more interesting in the Investigating Department, he thought as he edged through the doorway into the corridor beyond and moved at the regulation trot down the stairs towards the basement shelters.

And there at least he wouldn't have to crowd into the ordinary office shelters like this, taking fifteen minutes to get there and all the time wondering if the world was suddenly going to fry behind your back before the doors were shut. After all, the Investigating Department did most of its work underground anyway.

He sat on one of the crowded benches in the huge vaulted shelter, wondering how long it would be before the all clear went and he could get out again for a quick cigarette, and developed that sudden thought which had come to him when the alarm went. It was possible. Everything fitted.

She had gone back to get those pathetic underclothes. Suppose she had met with the bloke who had interrupted them? It could be him she was going to meet. The idea seemed slightly far-fetched, but it was the only answer which fitted all the facts.

And now he came to think of it for the first time, there had been something odd about that character. He'd said something, but it hadn't been English. He'd looked odd, too. What language had he spoken then? He wasn't sure, but it hadn't sounded like Chinese, and certainly the man had been far too big for a Chink.

Half an hour later when the all clear went, Nicol Snaith walked thoughtfully out of the shelter, convinced that there was something here which would repay investigation.

He hovered unobtrusively round the Typing Pool door at lunch time but saw no sign of her. She must have left pretty quickly, and he wished he knew where she was heading. He snatched a quick sandwich at the automatic canteen, not wanting to stand for hours in the counter queue at the cafeteria. Besides he knew from bitter experience that the cooked food was even less edible than usual on the day when an alarm had gone.

He took up his position again with a couple of wrapped ham sandwiches and a plastic cup of coffee and watched the door to the Typing Pool.

She returned at a couple of minutes to fourteen hundred hours, looking a little flushed as though she had been hurrying. She carried three books under her arm, and from the dull colour of the bindings he knew they had come from the public library.

He went back to his desk, wondering what to make of this. Possibly there was nothing in it at all, but if he ever wanted to become an Investigating Officer this was the sort of thing he would be expected to notice and to concern himself with. All right, even if there was

78

nothing in it, it would be a useful exercise for his future employment.

And then he froze, pen poised forgotten over another buff form.

If he no longer had the shapeless fool where he wanted her, how the hell was he ever going to get into the Investigating Department?

At last he shrugged. That would take care of itself in the future. In the meantime he would have to find out just exactly where he was with her.

6

Prudence left the house shortly after sunset. She had had a bath and doused herself liberally with the lilac-scented talcum powder which she had bought the previous day before meeting Nicky. She had washed her hair and done what she could to make its lank straightness look attractive, and she wore her best flower-print dress which Uncle Victor complained made her look like a Galashiels harlot. She was quite sure that Uncle Victor hadn't the remotest idea what—if anything—a Galashiels harlot was, but the suggestion suddenly took on a strangely attractive quality.

With the library books carefully tucked into a string bag she hurried along the road out of the Town Complex, and by the time darkness had really fallen she was making her way towards the fringe of trees at the base of the three hills.

He was waiting where she had left him the previous night, and her heart turned over with pleasure at the sight of him.

"*Salve*," she said a little breathlessly.

The moon had not yet risen and there was so little light under the trees that she could scarcely make him out, but she saw the flash of his teeth, and she gasped.

"Hello," he said in English, and she gasped.

"You——you *can* speak English," she said.

"I have spent the time since we last met learning it," he said. His accent was almost true, slightly liquid and careful in its enunciation, and there was a simplicity in his sentences which must have come from lack of a sufficient vocabulary and grammar, but to have progressed so far so fast was almost unbelievable.

"I'm glad," she said, deliberately sticking to simple words so that he might understand her more easily. "I have brought the books."

"Thank you," he said. "You are very kind."

"I shall have to return them to the library. When can I get them back?"

"Tomorrow night?"

"Will you have finished them so soon?"

"Yes. But I may have to ask you to get me some more."

"I'd be very pleased," she said shyly.

He laid a vast hand on her shoulder and without pausing to think she put up her own hand and laid it over his.

"You have been very helpful," he said softly. "You cannot know what solace you have brought me."

She stirred a little uncomfortably.

"I have done nothing," she said. "Anyone would do the same."

"What are you called?"

"Prudence Briggs."

"Prudencebriggs."

"No. Two words. Prudence. Briggs. People call me Prudence."

"Ah. Prudence. I understand. That is a word in your language which means good things. Carefulness. Wisdom. Gentleness. Is that not so?"

"Perhaps," she said, and laughed a little. "It doesn't mean that *I'm* any of those things."

80

"I think you are."

There was a silence which grew into something bigger than Prudence had expected and which frightened her a little. A sudden breeze rustled a nearby bush and the mood was broken. She was relieved and regretful at the same time. She had not noticed a breeze, but she probably wouldn't have noticed a thunderstorm.

"What are you called?" she asked.

"I'm called Trist."

"Just Trist?"

"That is my name."

"It's—unusual."

She saw the flash of his teeth again.

"So is yours," he said, and they laughed together and then were silent.

"You will want to read your books," she said a little regretfully.

He nodded.

"There is much work for me. I hope I can understand them. This metal must be found. Unless you have corenium I am helpless."

"Will you tell me why?"

"Not tonight," he said gently. "It would take too long. Perhaps tomorrow when you come for the books, or the next night when you bring me others, or the night after that when you take them back—?"

She laughed with a genuine gaiety which she had not felt for many years.

"Goodness, I must get some sleep sometime," she said.

"Of course you must."

She looked at him shyly and then reached up both her hands to his shoulders and began to draw him down. He bent over until his face was on the same level as hers. She looked into the depths of his eyes whose color she still could not tell, and then she kissed him gently on the mouth. He responded with equal gentleness and after only a few seconds they both drew apart.

He straightened up to his normal height again and looked down at her.

"We have that custom too," he said.

"I think it's universal."

He was silent for quite a while.

"I think you may be right," he said softly, and she thought she could detect an infinite sadness in his voice.

"Tomorrow night?" she said.

"Tomorrow night. Here."

For a moment more she looked at the dim figure in front of her, and then she turned and made her way out of the wood, heading towards the lights of the Town Complex.

7

Nicol Snaith strode into the Department Building through Number Twelve Entry, flashed his identity card at the sleepy duty officer, and took the lift to the seventeenth floor.

He had her now. And he had him, too. The conversation he had overheard in the wood had been enough. Bitch. Turning him down for a greasy foreigner like that. Well, by the time he'd finished she'd wish she'd never clapped eyes on the bloke. At least, if things worked out the way he hoped they would. And if they did he needn't go crawling after her any more, which would be a relief. There were more direct ways of getting into the Investigating Department.

The lift door sighed open and he strode along the brightly lit corridor to a door marked *Integrated Communications Unit*. In the room beyond, a large blocky piece of machinery filled the far wall. He paused in front of it for a moment and then pressed a key marked *Information*. The machine was linked to the Department of Employment and Productivity's central computer in which was stored details of every man, woman and child in the country.

T.R.I.S.T., he tapped out on the keyboard, wondering as he did so if that was the way you spelt the name. He could try possible variations later.

The machine hummed for a moment and then the teleprinter began to chatter.

He waited as the paper disgorged itself slowly. There was nothing much he could do until the machine had finished. But the name seemed unusual, so it shouldn't take long.

It didn't.

A minute later the machine fell silent and he ripped off the length of paper on which the message was printed.

There were eleven Trists listed in the computer's store, and he took the paper to a desk and sat down to study it. He now had their names, addresses, occupations, telephone numbers, ages, National Insurance numbers and all other details the Department required.

Five of the names he could discard straight away because they were women. Four others followed as being obviously under or over age. That left two, and they had the same address in South Devon which made it look as if they were brothers, and the date of birth seemed to confirm that.

He checked by telephone to make sure both these Trists were at home. They were. So neither could possibly be the one he had seen less than half an hour before with Prudence Briggs.

Carefully he covered every possible permutation in his spelling of the name and found no others.

Fine. That was just fine. The man Prudence Briggs

had fallen for instead of him was not listed in the Department's files. That was all he wanted to know.

He left the Integrated Communications Unit and returned to the lift, pressing the button for the sub-basement.

A minute later he was in the corridor twenty meters below ground level, and following the sign which directed him to the Investigating Department.

There was a burly-looking uniformed sergeant standing behind the public counter when he entered the Department's outer office. Snaith had a long walk from the door to the counter and the sergeant watched him unblinkingly all the way in a slightly unnerving manner. He continued to gaze at him after he had come to a stop, and Snaith's eyes eventually dropped uncomfortably.

"Well?" said the sergeant.

"Yes, well, look, I've found a spy," said Snaith.

The sergeant's expression remained the same as he drew a pad towards him and extracted a pen from his breast pocket.

"Name?" he asked.

"You mean—my name?"

The sergeant looked up slowly and contemptuously.

"Of course," he said.

Snaith gave it and his address and several other details the sergeant demanded.

"All right. Sit down over there," said the sergeant and turned and went through an inner door.

Snaith sat down on a hard wooden bench, feeling a sense of anticlimax. The sergeant had not even asked him for any details of the spy. It was almost as though he wasn't interested.

He sat and fidgeted for some time in the empty office. The sergeant returned and without a glance at him went back to work at the counter. Silence fell except for the occasional rustle as the sergeant turned over a sheet of paper. After something like twenty minutes a bell rang suddenly and the sergeant pushed aside the paper he had been writing on.

"Right," he said. "This way."

He opened the flap in the counter to allow Snaith to pass through, and then led the way through the inner door.

The passage beyond was narrow and as the door sighed shut behind them a curious stillness fell around them. Their feet made no noise on the soft composition flooring, and Snaith had the feeling that the whole place was soundproofed.

The sergeant opened a door a short distance down the passage and gestured him in in silence.

The man behind the desk was small with eyes which matched the iron-grey of his hair. His face was thin and as neat and uncrumpled as the plain dark grey suit he wore. The unblinking, hypnotic eyes stared at Snaith until his own dropped before them. Damn, he thought, why can't I meet these people as equals?

"Sit down, Snaith."

The voice was low-pitched with a hint of steel lurking in it, and Snaith hurriedly sat down in the chair on his side of the desk. The man opposite him looked down at a folder which, apart from the telephone, was the only thing lying on the desk top. He moved the folder fractionally with trim, well-kept hands until the bottom edge of it lay precisely along the edge of the desk. With a shock Snaith recognised his own name, upside down, on the cover.

"I am Commander Pearson. You have something you wish to tell us."

It was not a question, not even a statement. It was a command. Snaith began to talk hastily, words tripping over themselves to get out, and he stopped and tried to

85

pull himself together and speak more calmly, but the stillness of the man on the other side of the desk was very unnerving.

Suddenly his whole carefully constructed case against Prudence's stranger seemed full of holes and utterly unconvincing. His suspicion that the man was not English, the fact that he was looking for some unknown metal, the mystery of where he came from, the fact that he had no records in the Department of Productivity files all seemed hollow, and he felt defeated before he had finished telling his story.

Then Commander Pearson's questions started.

"This girl you—ah—took out last night. Her name?"

"Prudence Briggs. Social Security Sixth Typing Pool. Desk 319."

Pearson drew a gold pen from his pocket and made a neat note on a piece of paper in the folder.

"You feel there is no possibility that you may have misheard the man's name?"

"I don't think so."

"You checked the name with the computer?"

"Yes. It doesn't tally with any names on the files."

"You have some justification, I assume, for believing that Trist is the man's surname?"

"Of course . . . well, it sounds like a surname . . ."

"I agree it sounds like a surname. But do you think a girl meeting a man in a wood at night is likely to address him by his surname? Without even a 'Mr.' at the front?"

"Well, she might, especially if she doesn't know him—"

Snaith's voice trailed away as he began to see that his investigations had not been quite so thorough as they ought to have been. Pearson stared at him placidly for a moment and then switched his line of questioning.

"Now, let us think of the language this person used when you first saw him," he said.

"I don't know what it was. It wasn't English."

"Quite so. You have seen television films of the Chinese leaders. Did it sound like Chinese?"

"I don't know, I tell you! They were both speaking it . . ."

"I see. This metal he mentioned. Corenium. You're sure that's what he said?"

"That's what it sounded like."

"But you're not sure?"

"Look, how could I be? I never heard of corenium. I don't know anything about metals. That's what it sounded like, I'm telling you!"

Pearson smiled a little thinly.

"You don't believe me," said Snaith dully.

Pearson's eyes seemed to bore into him like twin gimlets.

"Oh, yes," he said. "I believe you. Your story is untested and uncorroborated. Nevertheless it has the ring of truth. But we need more help from you."

Snaith swallowed and plucked up his flagging courage.

"Listen," he said. "If I help you, will you do something for me in return?"

Pearson's eyebrows rose fractionally as though he was surprised.

"What had you in mind?" he asked softly.

"I—I'd like to join the Department," said Snaith.

Pearson stared at him for a long time and he began to fidget uncomfortably.

"That has nothing to do with me," Pearson said in the same quiet tone of voice. "The Department is always in need of men of the right calibre."

"If I do what you want now, will you put in a word for me?"

"We'll see," said Pearson after another discomforting pause. "Now listen carefully and I'll tell you what you have to do."

The alarm had gone and everyone was in the shelters, but for some reason Prudence was still outside. She was standing at the fringe of the trees looking out over the field. A swirling mist was rising from the ground in front of her, and in it she saw the huge figure of Trist. He was striding towards her, a welcoming smile on his face, his arms held out to her, and though she tried to move towards him she found her feet would not propel her forwards though they were working as hard as they would go. Then out of the mist rose hundreds upon thousands of Chinese, all dressed in their drab coveralls and caps, all looking exactly alike, slant eyes full of hate, mouths chanting unintelligible and meaningless slogans, each with a book in one hand and a sub-machine gun in the other. Trist did not seem to see them, and he came striding towards her.

Take cover, Trist, she thought desperately. *Oh, my dearest, be careful.*

And then the Chinese began to fire. *Tap, tap, tap* went the sub-machine guns and she saw the flare and sparkle of the bullets like a swarm of tiny fireflies. The look of happy expectancy on Trist's face changed to one of surprise, then of realization, then of pain, and she found her legs at last moving forward. But as she moved forward, Trist's movement slowed. She seemed to glide between the Chinese, whose mouthing faces floated past and behind her, and then she reached him.

The strange white suit was full of holes and his face looked questioningly at her, and suddenly she was kneeling on the ground with his head in her lap, stroking the crisp golden hair, and tears falling hot on his face which seemed to be glazing over.

Tap, tap, tap went the sub-machine guns, more

insistently than ever, although the Chinese seemed to have retreated. Then the mist, which was still rising from the ground, groped into her head and everything began to shimmer and go dim. She tried to call out to Trist, but no sound came, and the tap of the guns was louder than ever.

She woke in a bath of perspiration, the bedclothes a tangled mess and mostly off the bed, and it took her a second or two to reorientate herself.

Tap, tap, tap.

But it wasn't sub-machine guns. The wind must be rustling Uncle Victor's climbing rose against her bedroom window. And then she realized that there was no wind.

Head still swimming slightly she slipped out of bed, groped for her glasses and put them on while her feet located her slippers. She went to the window and drew aside the curtain.

Nicky was outside, hand raised to tap again. She frowned and opened the window.

"Nicky," she whispered, "what do you want? What time is it? Don't do that, you'll wake Uncle Victor."

"Sorry, doll," said Nicky hoarsely. "Listen, I wouldn't do this if it wasn't urgent."

"Can't it wait till the morning? I'm tired."

"No. Listen, doll, it's Trist."

Suddenly she was wide awake.

"What do you know about him?" she asked.

"Never mind about that. He wants you. It's very urgent."

"But how—? Where—?"

Just as suddenly her mind was confused again, memories of her recent dream conflicting with reality.

"Hurry, doll. I'll take you to him. But you got to be quick. Or you may be too late."

"But—All right. I'll dress—"

"No time for that. *Come on!*"

"All right. All right, I'm coming."

"Not out the door. Out the window."

"But—but why?"

"I'll explain as we go. Hurry. It's a matter of life and death."

He kept talking, urging her to hurry, giving her no time to think. Trist had needed her in her dream. Maybe he needed her in reality.

She climbed on to the window sill and dropped out, scratching her bare arm on Uncle Victor's climbing rose as she went, and Nicky caught her as she landed. Then he took her hand and began to lead her between Uncle Victor's house and the next door one towards the lane at the back.

"Nicky, what's happened?" she gasped.

"I'll tell you when we get there," he said shortly.

He pushed her through the gate at the bottom of the garden and closed it behind them. She turned to ask him which way they were to go, but the urgency seemed suddenly to have left him. He was standing with his back to the gate, and something in his attitude made her pause.

"Miss Briggs?" said a quiet voice beside her, and she whirled round.

A dim figure stood at her right shoulder, and she could make out the shape of a uniform cap against the night sky.

"What—?" she began.

"Investigating Department, Miss Briggs. We have some questions to ask you. Please come this way."

She began to protest, but another uniformed figure appeared at her other side and her elbow was grasped in a firm hand. She could feel the middle finger perilously close to the painful region of her funny bone and it seemed to constitute a warning.

"I—I don't understand," she said fearfully.

"You will, Miss Briggs. Come along."

90

Her heart was thumping now. This sort of thing used to happen many years ago in Germany with the Gestapo, she knew, and she had heard ugly rumors that it could sometimes happen here now. Certainly she knew as well as anyone else that the Investigating Department of the Ministry was to be avoided.

She looked back at Nicky, still standing by the closed gate behind which lay safety and security, and where Uncle Victor would be snoring gently, dreaming of the two medium boiled eggs which she would not be doing for him in the morning.

"Oh, Nicky," she said, shaking her head in disbelief. "What did you do it for?"

But the arms drew her away before he could reply.

9

Trist sat on the mossy bank under the trees and waited for Prudence Briggs. He was almost certain that the books she had brought had destroyed his last hope. Prudence's choice had been excellent. One had been an elementary school textbook on metallurgy, the second had been an enormous standard work on the subject published, it would seem, some time ago, and the third had been the most modern work she could find on the library shelves. The first had enabled him quickly to pick up the basics of the subject as they were understood on this planet, and the second had given him all the detail he needed. From these two he had become convinced that no such metal as the one he so desperately needed was known here, and the third had confirmed this view. If such a metal did exist it had not yet been discovered or manufactured, and in the planet's reasonably advanced state of metallurgical knowledge that seemed highly unlikely.

He looked up at the dark sky above him and wondered with a terrible sense of longing where up there lay Haven. If only he knew where his home was it might be easier to bear.

But then again, it might not. A thought had been buzzing insistently at the back of his mind, demanding attention, an attention which he had refused to allow it, for he knew that if he brought the thought into the open he would know the true meaning of despair.

Prudence Briggs had given him some idea of how long it had been since the Romans were in this land, and by equating her counting of time with his he knew that the sleep pill must have kept him unconscious for many generations. Which meant that Haven too would have changed, and that the *Revelation* and Captain Graud and his crewmates would not only have given up searching for him long ago, but would themselves be dead and forgotten.

Prudence Briggs was later than he expected, and suddenly he wanted her to be there, for she seemed the one sure point in a shifting universe, the one element of kindness and compassion and sympathy he had to hold on to, as yesterday he had held on to the physical warmth of her tiny hand. And he didn't even know what she really looked like. He had only met her in the dark, but the tone of her voice and the way she had willingly and unquestioningly fallen in with his needs was an element of comforting sanity.

He got to his feet and was suddenly blinded as a light shone directly into his eyes.

"All right, Trist," said a harsh voice from the pitch darkness beyond the light. "Put up your hands and don't move."

He screwed his eyes tight shut against the glare, and felt hands seize his arms. He opened his eyes, taking care not to look directly at the light, and saw shadowy forms moving around him, many of them carrying some kind of weapon, bigger than the stun gun he had left in the scout ship, deadly looking and ready for use.

His brain whirled frantically. Who were these people and why were they here, and why were they treating him as though he were dangerous?

He found himself being propelled out of the wood. He had not so far dared to venture far from the scout ship. The changes which he could see from his first expedition on this world had made him cautious. Where before there had been nothing but dense forest there were now cultivated fields ringing the suburbs of a huge and recently built town. In a few more days, with Prudence Brigg's help, he might have ventured into the streets of civilization to see what he could learn there. Now it seemed he was to be taken there in any case.

Creatures only use force when they are frightened or unsure of themselves. He could hear the sharp voice of Captain Graud speaking to the ship's company, and in all Haven's dealings with other worlds this precept seemed to hold good.

Therefore these people must be frightened, because they seemed perfectly sure of themselves. In which case what were they frightened of? Surely not him, for although he was very much bigger than they were, he had given them no cause for alarm.

They led him to a vehicle, though what kind of vehicle he could not make out very clearly in the darkness. It was noisy and smelly and extremely uncomfortable, but fortunately the journey did not last long.

He was hustled into a huge building, glowing with light from thousands of windows, and taken down in a form of elevator to some basement.

There followed an endless walk along corridors, round corners until he had totally lost his sense of direction, his guards marching stiffly beside him, weapons still at the ready, and eventually they stopped at a door.

One of his captors, who seemed to be some kind of officer by the different insignia on his uniform, opened the door, and he was pushed forward into the room beyond.

It was a small room with no window and only the one door.

A desk filled the far wall, and behind it sat three men. Trist eyed them curiously. One was clearly some kind of engineer. He wore a large pair of earphones and was fiddling with what looked like primitive recording gear. Another was a younger man whose narrow face had incipient acne and whose long hair curled round his shoulders. He too Trist dismissed as being unimportant, although his appearance struck a slight chord of recognition in his mind. It was the third man, sitting in the central position, who merited consideration. A small man, neatly dressed, with short, iron-grey hair and iron-grey eyes, and a face devoid of all expression.

The door thudded shut behind him and he stood facing the desk.

"Name," said the iron-grey man quietly.

"Trist."

"Other names."

"I have no other names."

The man stared at him in silence.

"How do you spell Trist?"

"I have no idea how you would spell it. I can only pronounce it for you."

"What is your National Insurance number?"

"I don't understand what you mean."

The iron-grey man smiled a little grimly.

"I see," he said. "Where do you come from?"

Something made Trist pause. These men were hostile, he knew that, and they were frightened. If he told them the truth, that he had come from a far-distant planet, he could foresee one of two different reactions. They might believe him. If they did, it seemed logical to

94

assume that they would treat him as an enemy. He had the feeling that anything they did not understand they would regard as being unfriendly. But the chances were they would not believe him, and he wondered what they might do to get at what they thought was the truth.

"I come from far away," he said.

The iron-grey man's smile seemed to become grimmer.

"We deduced that," he said. "Exactly where?"

"May I ask you a question?"

"You may not."

"Why do you wish to know?"

"I said no questions."

"Well, no questions, no answers."

"Let me put the case to you. You are found lurking in the trees at the foot of the Eildon Hills. Your knowledge of English is sufficiently poor to show that it is not your native language. You have no records —under the name you give, at least—in the Department of Employment and Productivity files. You appear not to know what a National Insurance number is. You are making enquiries about a mysterious metal called, I believe, corenium. Do you not feel that these circumstances are highly suspicious?"

"Not really," said Trist.

The man leaned forward on the desk and clasped his hands neatly in front of him.

"May I remind you that you are facing a Grade One interrogation by the Investigating Department."

Trist raised his eyebrows in polite enquiry, and the man grunted.

"It would seem that you are unaware of the Department's functions. Let me remind you of them. The Investigating Department was set up many years ago to uncover fraudulent misuse of the Welfare Services. That function has now been extended to trace persons who have no Social Security registration. Such people are usually here for the express purpose of spying."

Trist continued to look politely interested. The man was talking in terms which he could not follow, but he had no wish to appear ignorant.

"You have come here in order to find out what we know about this metal corenium," said the iron-grey man. "I should be interested to know exactly why you wish this knowledge."

Trist remained silent. The atmosphere of hostility had grown and for the first time he began to fear for his safety. And another thought had entered his mind. They knew about his need for corenium. The only person he had told about corenium had been Prudence Briggs. And she had not turned up to meet him earlier this evening. Could it be that for some reason she had told these authorities, whoever they were, about him? He refused to believe that. She couldn't have done! It was more likely that they must have grown suspicious of her and treated her in much the same way as they were treating him.

The iron-grey man was still talking.

"I am going to be frank with you. We know nothing whatever of this metal you are asking about. At least not under the name of corenium. However, it is possible that we *do* know of it under some other name. We shall only be able to establish this if you will give us the basic elements of the metal."

In spite of the even tone of the voice which had not varied since he had been brought into the room, Trist had the feeling that this was the climax. The long-haired man was staring at him with thinly veiled expectancy. There was an oppressive silence in the room, and then the iron-grey man stirred slightly and began to speak again.

"Let us be quite clear on one thing," he said. "Your days of espionage are over. Who you are and where you come from are really immaterial. I presume you are working for the Chinese. This we shall discover at our leisure. However, you must understand that if the Chinese have access to a metal unknown to us, we naturally want to find out all we can about it. And that is why you are here. We shall find out from you."

Trist shook his head. There was an underlying note of menace in the smooth voice now which confirmed his decision to say nothing about where he came from. These people were still savages underneath their thin veil of civilization, and from what he could make out they were still at each others' throats in the way the Picts and the Romans had been. It would be unwise to tell them anything.

"Oh, but we shall, make no mistake about it," went on that level voice. "It would make life much easier for everyone if you would simply tell us now."

Trist smiled wryly. How could he tell them? He had had difficulty enough in unravelling their methods of describing metal from the books Prudence Briggs had brought, and he had had to use the scout ship's miniature computer to help him with the language and to decode the symbols. He was fairly sure that these people would not understand *his* symbols and would not have a technique sufficiently advanced to interpret them.

"You will tell us eventually, you know," said the iron-grey man.

In the silence one of the guards behind him shifted his feet, and the scuff of his heel on the soft composition flooring seemed unnaturally loud.

"Very well," said the iron-grey man. "Bring her in."

One of the guards opened the door and Trist turned. Two more guards came in, supporting Prudence Briggs.

Trist took a step towards her, but one of his guards raised his gun threateningly and he stopped.

Her feet shuffled listlessly along the floor. She was

barefoot and wore a short, flimsy pink garment with a flowery belt at the waist. Her shoulders were bowed and her face was drawn with an unutterable weariness. Without her glasses she looked strangely defenseless and her eyes were glazed and unseeing.

"Your accomplice has been questioned thoroughly," said the even voice behind him. "She had little to say, but she is still useful."

"What have you done with her?" Trist asked in horror. It was not that she was injured or marked in any way. It was just that she seemed drained of all life.

"Nothing very much. She has been questioned continuously for thirty-six hours. She will not sleep until you tell us about corenium."

"Prudence," he said, and this time he ignored the threatening guns and went to her, putting his hands on the bowed shoulders. "Prudence what have they done to you?"

She stirred and blinked tiredly. Her eyes hunted around, vague and unfocused, and then came to rest on him. Recognition dawned slowly in her face.

"Trist," she whispered hoarsely. "Oh, my poor Trist. They've caught you."

Tears welled in her eyes and began to roll unheeded down her cheeks.

"I—I'm sorry. I—I didn't tell them anything. There wasn't anything I could tell them, Trist. I—I think they know that now. But they won't let me sleep and I'm so tired. I just want—to sleep—"

Her head dropped forward suddenly, and one of the guards beside her shook her arm roughly and she jerked upright.

Trist felt himself trembling with fury.

"Is this the way you treat your people?" he demanded, whirling back to the desk.

The iron-grey man looked steadily at him.

"It is unfortunate but sometimes necessary. In any

case, yours do worse. Take her away."

The guards turned her round and guided her out of the room and the door closed softly behind them.

"She will be allowed to sleep as soon as you tell us about corenium," said the iron-grey man. "If you decide to remain stubborn then we must with great reluctance consider what further measures may be employed upon her to make you speak."

Trist clenched his hands and tried to calm the rage which was welling in him. Careful, he thought. These people were mad. He might manage to break the iron-grey man in two before he was gunned down by the guards, but that wouldn't help either him or Prudence.

"We shall meet again at nine hundred hours," said the iron-grey man. "I trust you will have reached a wise decision by then. But rest assured that Prudence Briggs will not sleep in the meantime. Take him away."

And the iron-grey man unclasped his hands, stood slowly and turned away as though he had already lost interest in the proceedings, and Trist found himself being escorted from the room.

10

He lay on the hard bunk, the rough blanket drawn over him, and found his mind tackling two separate problems.

In the first place he was listening to the feet of the guard outside his cell. There was a spyhole in the door, and once every ten minutes that spyhole clicked and an eye peered through at him. It was almost regular, never varying by more than a few seconds, and he knew in advance when it was going to happen because the guard had a squeaky boot. He filed this information away while he examined the cell. It was a small, bare room. There was a window in the wall opposite the door with heavy bars running up and down it. He was still on the same level as the room where he had been questioned, so he assumed that the ground must slope downwards towards this side of the building. The light was on and there was no switch to turn it off. Apart from the bunk there was a strangely shaped receptable in one corner which he assumed was for personal relief, and a chair in another.

Secondly his mind was busy trying to understand the background of these people. It seemed unbelievable that on so small a planet they could be warring with each other, and yet all the evidence he had collected pointed in that direction. It was something unknown on Haven, and he wondered what could have caused the difference. Possibly a basic variation in the two different types of animal, though on the surface it was difficult to see any variations at all. He was very much bigger than the people of this planet, but that was a minor detail.

He tried to compare what he had discovered here with life on Haven and found it very difficult, for he had little experience of this planet. But it seemed that there was a strange dichotomy. On the one hand there was fear and danger of war, and on the other there was the Welfare State Prudence had told him about and which the iron-grey man had mentioned. From what Trist had gathered, everyone was so coddled and fondled under this system that there was nothing to attract the inventiveness of the people, nothing for them to challenge except each other. On Haven there was plenty of challenge. There was the still hostile environment of parts of the huge planet, there were the nearby stars and planetary systems to establish contact and trade with. Trist's people could channel their energies constructively. On this planet it seemed the people could not. Maybe this didn't apply to the whole planet, and undoubtedly it was too simplified an explanation, but there was a certain logic in his concept.

The spyhole clicked and then clicked again, and he heard the squeaky boot of the guard fade down the corridor outside.

He had to get out of this madhouse and back to the sanity of the scout ship, and his plan was already formed in his mind. As soon as he heard the second click he flung back the blanket and stripped off his outer suit. He arranged it quickly on the hard bunk and pulled the blanket over it, covering it completely. The suit maintained its shape and at a cursory glance from the spyhole he was reasonably sure it would pass. He stood in his undersuit at the window and seized the two bars in his hands. He exerted pressure. The muscles strained and cracked across his shoulder and in his biceps and the concrete of the window frame powdered as the bars gradually pulled loose and bent apart. He blessed the extra strength he had on this planet. He climbed on to the chair and leapt for the window sill, pulling himself up and sliding through head first.

The ground was only a few feet below him and he landed and rolled upright in one movement, the lower gravity making it simple. He reached up and bent the bars as straight as he could across the window again. That should give him a lot longer before his escape was discovered.

Now the problem was to find his way back to the ship.

He was standing in a kind of yard surrounded by a low wall, and he crept along in the shadow of the building to a corner and peered round.

He stood for some time until he was sure there was no guard outside. Almost straight ahead of him, edged against the starry sky, were the familiar shapes of the three hills at the foot of which lay the scout ship.

He slipped across the yard and reached the safety of

the houses beyond. The street lighting was bright but there was no one around, which was hardly surprising as it must have been very late.

It was ludicrously easy. Half an hour later he was making his way through the trees to the spot where the scout ship was hidden. He reached the tangle of undergrowth, pulled aside the bush which hid the tunnel entrance and crawled in.

Down the narrow earthen passage which he had dug to get out when he awoke he came to the hatch of the scout ship, buried deep below the ground by age upon age of weathering and earth movement. He opened the hatch and crawled in, stretching himself out on the couch.

It was a relief to be back, however alone and cut off he seemed here. He wanted nothing more to do with these crazy creatures he had met with during the past night. If they were representative of the whole species there would be little hope indeed.

But they couldn't be representative. It was dangerous to generalize about any people. There was Prudence Briggs. She was different. For a moment he had wondered if for some reason she had betrayed him, but the sight of her in the interrogation room had killed that idea.

And suddenly he sat up on the couch. It had all seemed too easy. So easy that he had half suspected there must be a snag somewhere. There was. Prudence Briggs was still a prisoner.

Trist sat quite still for a few moments and then cursed suddenly and fluently. He couldn't leave her to the tender mercies of these people.

He opened the locker and took out the stun gun and checked to make sure its energy chamber was fully loaded. It was, which was fortunate, because the scout ship carried no refills.

He also took out the first aid box, opened it and

102

selected a capsule. He slipped it into his pocket and then undogged the hatch and crawled out of the scout ship again. He hoped the bars on his cell window would bear the strain of being bent twice more . . .

11

Nicol Snaith entered the interrogation room reluctantly the following morning. It was empty, save for the technician who was fitting a new spool of tape to his recorder. Snaith nodded to him and received a nod in reply. Was that nod contemptuous, he wondered, or was it nothing more than a nod? He could not be sure.

His feelings were strangely mixed. Here he was, allowed to sit in on an Investigating Department Grade One interrogation with Commander Pearson, one of the top men of this area. Not many people had had this privilege. He should have been bubbling over with pride.

Yet he wasn't. Partly he knew it was because of Pearson's attitude to him which consisted of thinly veiled contempt. Of course, he realized that was Pearson's attitude to most people and he should not read too much into it.

He wondered if Trist would have seen sense overnight. He rather hoped so. Pearson had left him in no doubt of what would happen to Prudence if Trist proved recalcitrant, and Snaith felt his stomach turn slightly at the thought. Not that he particularly cared what happened to Prudence. Silly blind bitch, if she'd had the sense to stick to him instead of throwing herself at this big muscular oaf, she'd have been all right. He still had a smouldering resentment at her attitude. No, what really made him feel slighty queasy was the fact that he might have to witness the process which was being planned for her, and somehow he doubted if his stomach would stand the strain. It was terribly undignified if he threw up in front of Pearson. That would finish his prospects with the Investigating Department. If, he thought gloomily, he had ever really had any prospects in the first place. He had the uncomfortable feeling that he was only here because Pearson was honoring his side of the bargain in return for having Prudence brought in quietly and without fuss.

Pearson came smoothly into the room and said good morning to him and to the technician. Snaith could detect no difference in his tone of voice, and wondered whether this was a good thing or not. Pearson took his place at the desk and gestured Snaith to sit down. The technician finished fiddling with his equipment, nodded briefly, and Pearson pressed the buzzer on the desk in front of him, and then laid down his folder, placing the bottom edge of it neatly along the edge of the desk.

Snaith swallowed and tried to make his stomach settle. He lolled back in his chair in an attitude which he hoped suggested indolent boredom and wished he could light a cigarette, but Pearson didn't smoke and there were no ash-trays in the room, so he presumed it wasn't allowed.

"Don't slouch," said Pearson evenly. "Keep your dignity."

Snaith hastily sat up as the door opened and Trist came in, followed by two armed guards.

Trist stopped in front of the desk and stared at Pearson speculatively. Snaith wished the big man would look at him, acknowledge his presence in some way, but he might as well not have been there as far as Trist was concerned. Bastard. Well, he'd get what was coming to him.

"Have you thought over your attitude?" asked Pearson quietly.

"I have," said Trist.

"Then I trust you are prepared to cooperate now."

"I am prepared to cooperate on several conditions."

"You are in no position to make conditions."

"I think I am. You want information from me. In order to get that information you are prepared to go to barbaric lengths, and so I must presume that the information you want will in all probability be used for barbaric purposes. This I am not prepared to help you with. If you can prove to my satisfaction that the information is needed for constructive reasons only, then I should be happy to cooperate."

Pearson looked at him for a long time, his neat hands neatly clasped on the folder in front of him.

"I had hoped this might be avoided," he said, and he pressed the buzzer on the desk again. "I warned you last night of what would happen if you proved difficult. The girl will suffer first."

"I warn you not to touch her," said Trist evenly. "It will go badly with you if you do."

Pearson smiled thinly and said nothing.

The door opened and two guards half carried Prudence into the room. She seemed hardly able to stand although her legs were making curious movements as though they were trying to walk and not succeeding very well. The guards stood supporting her, and Snaith could see that if they let go she would fall. God, he thought, she looks a wreck. Even more so than usual. She slumped in the guards' arms, and they shook her violently so that her head wagged like a rag doll's. One of the guards grasped her hair and forced her head back, and the other slapped her hard across the cheeks. The eyes opened, unfocussed, glassy without glasses, and her mouth hung open. A thin dribble of saliva coursed down her chin. Snaith turned his eyes away. It made him squeamish to look at her.

He looked at Trist instead. The big man's face had gone white and the muscles round his mouth had tensed. Snaith shivered suddenly. This man could be dangerous if he lost his temper, and it looked as if he were perilously close to doing so now. However, the guards were armed and he was unlikely to try anything stupid.

"You will tell us all you know about corenium," said Pearson quietly.

"No," said Trist between clenched teeth.

"Very well," said Pearson, and he turned and nodded to the guards holding Prudence.

One of them seized both her arms and held her in front of him. The other, freed now, took one of her limp hands and held it in one of his own. He produced a pin from the lapel of his uniform and then very deliberately inserted it between the nail and the flesh of her middle finger and pushed.

The room suddenly reverberated with her scream of pain and Snaith found himself deafened. He saw Prudence slump forward as though she had fainted, and then he was leaning forward, his stomach heaving uncontrollably, and he vomited all over the desk.

12

The scream distracted the attention of those in the room for just long enough to give Trist his chance. He took a step backwards bringing his flanking guards in front of him, and before they had registered his action he reached out his arms, seized each of them round the neck and brought their heads together with a crack which he could feel shiver up to his shoulders.

As they dropped to the floor he pulled the stun gun from his pocket, flipped it to narrow beam maximum, and fired at the guard who had used the pin on Prudence. There was a hiss and the man crumpled.

The guard who held Prudence had to release her to

go for his weapon, and as soon as he let go she fell, leaving him totally exposed. Trist fired again and the man went down.

He whirled and brought the butt of the gun down hard on the iron-grey man's hand just as he was reaching for the buzzer on the desk. The man gasped with pain as the bones in his hand cracked, and Trist raised the gun again and brought it crashing down on his head.

Out of the corner of his eye he noticed that the technician had backed away from the desk, eyes terrified, hands held high, and the long-haired man on the other side was too busy being sick to be a danger at the moment. Nevertheless he adjusted the gun to minimum and fired at both of them. The technician folded up, his hands still held high, and the awful retching noise suddenly ceased as the long-haired man slumped forward.

Trist stood for a moment breathing heavily, stomach queasy at the sour stench of vomit in the room, his eyes taking in the scene. The long-haired man and the technician would recover within half an hour. The two guards he had gunned would take four times as long. He had no idea about the first two but from the cracks their heads had received they would be the last to recover. He looked at the iron-grey man. He would not waken at all. Trist must have hit him too hard, for the back of his head was soft and pulpy. Strength was hard to gauge in this unaccustomed gravity.

He pushed the stun gun back into his pocket and went down on his knees to Prudence. She was lying where she had fallen and appeared to be in a deep sleep. He shook her gently by the shoulder and she stirred slightly and moaned.

"Wake up," he said insistently. "Prudence. Wake up. Please. It's Trist. Wake up."

She stirred again, and one hand made a futile

sweeping motion as though she were trying to brush away a disturbance.

He kept on talking as he felt in his pocket and produced the capsule he had brought from the scout ship. She opened her eyes and blinked and shook her head and tried to turn over and go back to sleep again, but he wouldn't let her. He kept talking, shaking, telling her to waken and at last the persistence of his voice and his actions got through to her and she was awake. Uncoordinated and only functioning at a fraction of her normal rate, but quite definitely awake.

"Prudence," he said. "Swallow this. It will help you for an hour or so. Trust me. Swallow it."

She moaned questioningly and tried to turn her mouth away, but he was firm and forced the capsule between her lips. He massaged her throat to help her swallow it and eventually he felt it go.

Good. Give her a few minutes for it to take effect.

Three minutes later she began to sit up, blinking rapidly, and at last she seemed aware of her surroundings.

"Trist," she said hoarsely. "Oh, Trist. You're all right?"

"I'm all right," he said. "We must hurry, Prudence. We must get out of here."

The urgency in his voice made her look round, her shortsighted eyes peering to take in the scene in the interrogation room. They widened in amazement.

"How—how?" she began, and he held up a hand.

"We have no time now," he said. "The drug I have given you will only last an hour. Then it will lose its power and you will have to sleep for a long time. By then we must be well away from here. Are you ready to go?"

She nodded almost happily and took his hand trustingly.

"Yes," she said. "So long as you are here."

108

"Good. Come with me, then."

"Where are we going?"

"You'll see."

He opened the door and glanced cautiously up and down the passage. There was no one in sight. He drew her out of the room and closed the door behind them. Turning left he set off, trying to recall the route he had taken this morning when he had been brought from his cell. Halfway between the cell and the interrogation room they reached lift doors. Trist summoned the lift and waited, every sense alert.

The doors sighed open and they stepped in. Trist pressed the ground button and the doors closed and they were lifted upwards. He glanced at Prudence. Her eyes were unnaturally bright and a hectic flush had appeared on her cheeks. The effects of the capsule, he thought, and hoped it would last long enough. If only she had had on some more appropriate clothing, for he was certain what she was wearing would attract attention. He knew his own clothing and his unnatural size would do the same, of course, but there was nothing he could do about it.

The door opened and he smiled at her. She smiled back quite happily, the drug mercifully muffling the high degree of tension she should normally have been experiencing.

They stepped out, and a quick glance showed that they had arrived at an unfrequented cross-corridor and there was no one in sight. So far so good, but Trist knew that they must come to a more populated area the closer they came to an exit.

They seemed fairly lucky. It was about half past nine in the morning and the traffic into the building had almost ceased. They came to the Number Eight Entry without meeting anyone, but a few people were hanging around the entry hall and the duty officer was sitting at his desk reading a paper.

Trist paused and glanced at Prudence. She looked at him expectantly out of those unnaturally bright eyes, and he nodded and took her hand.

"Come on," he said.

They slipped unobtrusively into the hall. At first no one paid them any attention. The few people standing in the hall seemed intent on their own business, and the duty officer had not noticed them. They were within three paces of the door when he spoke.

"Er—just a minute, sir," he called.

Trist squeezed Prudence's hand and strode on without a pause as though he hadn't heard.

The duty officer spoke again more insistently, and at the sound of his voice some of the people began to look round. Trist noticed one of them staring in amazement at their strange dress.

Then they were outside and the door swung shut behind them. Trist breathed a sigh of relief.

"Just keep walking naturally," he said.

They were half way across the yard when the bell suddenly screamed into life on the wall of the building, making his heart leap. It sounded so like the scout ship alarm that he found his hand half way up to close his non-existent face-plate in an instinctive reaction. But danger was not coming from that direction.

"Come on—quick!" he said.

He tried to hurry her across the yard, but Prudence seemed to have fallen into a steady rhythm of action and it was as if the drug would not allow her to change it. She resisted his pull.

Behind them voices began calling on them to stop. Trist kept going, heading for a corner of the nearest building. Once behind that they might be safe, but at the moment they were horribly exposed.

There was a sudden crack and something whined past just over his head. They were firing.

It was like a nightmare trying to get Prudence to

increase her pace. This wouldn't do. Unless he could get her to move faster they had no chance.

There was another crack and he stopped as he saw Prudence stagger and the calm, bright look on her face turned to one of dull surprise. She half leaned against him and coughed.

Blood appeared at the corner of her mouth.

For a split second he stared at her without moving, and then he gathered her into his arms as gently as he could and set off for the corner, running far faster than they had been going before. She seemed extraordinarily light in his arms.

He reached the corner and slipped round it as a further flurry of bullets sprayed round them, shattering pieces of stonework off the building.

But he could not slow down. The exit they had used had brought them out at the wrong side of the building. In order to get back to the scout ship he would have to reverse direction, and that would mean going through populous parts of the Town Complex, and the Investigating Department guards would have them before he had gone any distance at all.

And there were people here. Far too many people, getting in the way, questioning, curious. They seemed to be gathering round him, impeding his progress, and behind him now he could hear the shouts of the guards calling on him to stop.

He dodged down another side road, and then another, until he was totally lost in a maze of streets, all with identical houses on both sides. He had lost his sense of direction and if he was not careful he could double back and run into the men who were pursuing them.

And then the alarm went.

He thought it was another signal set off because of their escape, but suddenly everyone in the streets seemed to lose interest in them.

He did not understand why, but in a matter of a minute the streets were empty and silent. Cautiously he slowed to a walk and then as the pursuit still did not materialize he stopped altogether.

In his arms Prudence had closed her eyes. The blood had spread now and was staining the white of his suit.

Carefully he put her down on the pavement and felt her pulse. It was weak and irregular, her breathing shallow and painful, and he was sure that the bullet must have entered a lung.

He felt a sense of helpless fury building up inside him, but his hands were gentle as he wiped the blood away from her mouth with a corner of her gown. The deep crimson contrasted horribly with the delicate pink of the material.

She stirred and opened her eyes. The brightness had gone from them, but mercifully the drug must still have been keeping pain away.

"My glasses," she breathed. "I can't see—"

"It's all right," he said gently.

"Trist? Where are you . . . ?"

"I'm here."

"I heard the alarm. You should—take cover."

"I'm all right."

She tried to sit up, but her movement was very weak and he took her gently and laid her head in his lap.

"You must," she said, and her voice was strained and she could hardly put two words together without drawing a shudderingly difficult breath. "Hydrogen bombs—cobalt—the Chinese—they'll kill you. They'll kill all of us—we must—get shelter—get a shelter, Trist—"

"It's all right," he said soothingly. "There's nothing to worry about."

"They'll shoot—tap, tap, tap—sub-machine guns —Oh, Trist my darling, be careful—"

He looked round helplessly. She was going fast. There was no chance of getting her to the scout ship in time, and even if he did he had not the materials to do anything for her.

"Where are we going, Trist—Where are you taking me?"

He stroked the lank hair gently and began to tell her about Haven, and his people and the lives they led. Of the sun and warmth of Haven and the purposefulness of its people. Of the worlds they had to explore and visit. He told her of his parents, tilling their farm in the moist uplands of the central region, and the deep satisfaction of reclaiming more and more land each year. Of his sister and two brothers who worked on the farm. Of himself, the only black sheep of the family, who had gone into the space service. He spoke of them as though they were still alive after all this time, and as he did so they became real again to him as he saw the acceptance of his story in the fading eyes of the dying girl.

"Are we going there, Trist? Is that where you're taking me?"

He nodded, feeling his throat tight, and she could no longer see the gesture and she asked the question painfully again.

"Yes," he said, lying gently to her. "That's where I'm taking you. You'll like it there."

"Yes," she said. "I will. So long as you're with me—don't leave me, Trist. I don't—want to be alone again—"

Her hand tightened momentarily on his and then relaxed and she turned away with a tired sigh.

He knelt where he was for some time, his throat sore and his vision blurred. Then he laid her on the ground and gently closed her eyes and stood up.

He wondered what he should do. He knew little of the customs of these people, and they could do her

113

neither physical nor mental harm now. It would be best to leave her to them.

He stood for a moment, head bowed, then turned away and strode off along the street. It was still silent and deserted, but it would have made little difference to him if it had been crowded as he made his solitary way back to the scout ship in the hills.

INTERLUDE

Trist stared blindly out of the forward viewport. Not that there was anything to see, for the port was still opaqued. Even had it not been there was only a vista of brown earth beyond. But Trist was seeing enough without that added reminder of the dead.

No corenium. Therefore no return to Haven. And even if he had been able to return to Haven what would he have found? His friends and relatives long dead and forgotten, his civilization crumbled. Was there any point in returning now?

He was probably better off in the scout ship, sealed into the monument of a dead culture's aspirations. At least here there was tangible memory of what his people had done, the greatness to which they had aspired, even if there was also a reminder of the dust to which they had inevitably fallen.

The radio was silent. His distress call had never been answered. It would not be answered now by anyone. Although it was alive, the shifting land mass had covered the aerial long ago, and not even waves from this planet were getting through the thick layer of earth around the ship.

Hopelessly he reached out a hand and switched it off.

He was beginning to get some concept of time here. Prudence had recited to him the seconds, minutes, hours, days, weeks, months and years by which these people counted, and his rough calculations showed that the planet's orbit round its primary was virtually equal to Haven's, though it spun faster on its axis. Three hundred and sixty five days in a year. And by his reckoning he had been awake now for just over five days.

Prudence had told him something of the Romans. They had flourished in this country up to about sixteen hundred years ago . . .

That was a long time.

Prudence . . .

He screwed up his eyes at the memory of her. All right, he had been condemning these people for their callousness, their stupidity, their lack of individuality and their lack of compassion. Probably there was some truth in that. And yet Prudence had given the lie to it all.

She had not been callous or stupid, and there had been an appealing innocence about her and a simple compassion which had touched him very deeply.

But she had died at the hands of the authorities. Was there something symbolic in that?

In any case, he had been cut off from contact with these people. He could not go back to them. Neither could they reach him, for he had collapsed the entry tunnel behind him. Therefore there was only one way he could go, and that was forward.

He opened the locker and took out Greet's sleep pill.

There were two alternatives open to him. Either he could end everything quietly and painlessly now, or he could take this last capsule and see what happened when he reawoke, whenever that might be. There was always the possibility that people of the next time would have managed to avoid the problems they were creating for themselves now, and to have advanced to such a stage that they would have discovered corenium or something equally effective.

If not he could take the death pill then.

But corenium was still important. With it he might be able to go home to Haven and at least die there where his own people had died.

116

He put on his helmet. It might be that when he reawoke he would need the small supply of oxygen still in his pack until he could dig a way out of the scout ship again.

He settled himself comfortably on the couch and put the capsule in his mouth.

THREE

1

Selena pushed herself off her knees and squatted back in a more comfortable position. This was strictly forbidden. She knew that she was supposed to remain kneeling during her two hour spell in the temple and to think purifying thoughts. But no one would know, and she simply had to ease the strain of tired muscles, and her thoughts were not purifying anyway.

They were principally of the fact that she was bored to tears.

She glanced round the temple with distaste. It was a big room, its metal walls covered with intricately designed hangings of luxurious unnatural fibers, carefully dyed in contrasting colors and cunningly lit by hidden strips. Its floor was covered with richly decorated rugs, the painstaking work of the Fine Arts Department. It was very quiet and dignified and impressive—and dull.

She sighed deeply and cradled her chin in one hand and stared at the catafalque in front of her.

There must always be a guard on the catafalque, the elders said, and she and the other Naturals had to take it in turns to watch over it. Now with the death in quick succession of four of the oldest Naturals in the last two weeks these spells of duty had been extended for those remaining, and what had formerly been one hour's duty

117

a day had suddenly become two hours every day and a half.

It had been bad enough trying to think purifying thoughts for an hour a day, but this was much worse.

And at the back of her mind she had a rebellious desire *not* to think purifying thoughts. Why should she? Was it her fault that she was a Natural? What was so wrong in being a Natural anyway? Oh, she saw the dangers as well as anyone, but none of the Naturals ever seemed to suffer from the dangers the elders kept bleating about.

She pushed her long hair back from her eyes and wished she was allowed to wear a ribbon of some kind to keep it out of the way, but that was strictly forbidden.

These thoughts had been occupying her mind to an increasing extent recently and she was slightly worried by them. After all, it seemed only a short step from thinking them to saying them out loud, and that would be terrible.

Maybe if the temple wasn't here it would make life easier. Then at least there would be nothing to keep watch on or think purifying thoughts over, but she supposed that the elders would find some other and perhaps less pleasant way of treating the Naturals.

Her calf muscles began to ache and she sank down to her knees again, seeing that they were now rested.

It was all such a *bore!*

In a fit of rebelliousness stronger than usual she stuck her tongue out at the catafalque which seemed to be the focal point of all her troubles.

2

There was a pinpoint of light, so small it was hardly noticeable. Then it began to expand, and as it expanded it increased its rate of expansion, so that it seemed suddenly that his field of vision had cleared.

He opened his eyes.

The ship had gone. There were strange shadows and strange lights in strange places. And he was lying on something much harder than his couch in a room. An empty room. No. Not quite empty.

Just within his field of vision a naked girl knelt on the floor, her face screwed up and her tongue stuck out at him.

He blinked in amazement, and watched the tongue suddenly withdrawn and the face smooth itself out, an answering amazement reflected in her eyes.

She leapt to her feet with a gasp, looked wildly round and then ran to a corner of the room.

"No. Wait a minute!" he called.

And she stopped and turned back obediently.

For a moment the significance escaped him. There was too much that was new and strange for his mind to accept. Had he spoken in his own language? Or had he spoken in English? or in Latin? Or even in the guttural tongue of the Picts? He thought it had been his own, but as the last mists of sleep cleared from his brain it was possible that he had used English without quite realising it. This time he made a conscious effort and spoke in his own language.

"Come here," he said.

For a moment she hesitated and then she began slowly to approach him, her eyes wide with speculation and a touch of awe as well.

She had understood him.

"Say something to me," he said.

Her mouth opened once or twice, and then she cleared her throat and spoke.

"What shall I say, lord?" she asked.

He frowned. She spoke in his language too! The accent was totally different but basically it was the same language. He felt his mind whirl.

She must have noticed his frown for she backed away.

"The Lord is angry," she said, trembling a little.

For a moment he forgot the language problem and smiled at her.

"Not I," he said. "Come and sit down."

"It is not permitted to sit in the Lord's presence."

"Well, the Lord tells you to sit down," he said and he swung his legs off the catafalque on which he had been lying and patted the stonework beside him. She approached cautiously and perched herself precariously on the edge.

For a moment he looked at her and felt a deep warmth begin to glow inside him, such a feeling as he had not known for many, many years.

She was very beautiful, and totally unembarrassed by her nakedness.

Her face was frank and open, perfectly oval and framed with long dark hair which hung to her shoulders. Wide brown eyes stared wonderingly into his. Her nose was slightly tilted, giving her face a look of suppressed impertinence, and her open mouth with the full red lips showed the whiteness of perfect teeth. She was tall, or so he judged from his previous experience of these people, with long supple legs, a narrow waist with a deep-set navel shadowed in the lights from the ceiling of the room, and perfect rounded breasts in which the aureoles of her nipples seemed to glow with rosy life.

"What's your name?" he asked.

"I am called Selena, Lord."

"I am not a Lord," said Trist. "I am just a man. My name is Trist."

"Yes, Lord."

Trist swallowed and turned away.

"Listen, Selena, haven't you got any clothes to put

120

on? I find it very difficult to concentrate at the moment."

"Oh, no, Lord. I couldn't," she said, her tone shocked.

"Why not?"

"It is forbidden. No Natural may enter the temple clothed. It would be unclean and not fitting."

"Who says so?"

"The elders say so, Lord."

"The elders . . . ? What is this place?"

"This is the Lord's temple."

"You mean *my* temple?"

"Yes, Lord."

"All right. Let that pass just now. What are you doing in my temple?"

"I and people like me must guard the Lord at all times."

"Are there more like you?"

"There are eighteen Naturals. Some are men, some are women, some are old, some are young, but all combine in the service of the Lord's temple. And now I must summon the elders——"

"Just a minute. Sticking out your tongue is a rude thing to do where I come from."

Selena blushed and suddenly began to concentrate very hard on the design her finger was tracing on the stonework of the pedestal.

"Isn't it the same with you?" he persisted.

After a moment she nodded. He couldn't see her face, for it was bowed and hidden by the curtain of her hair.

"Yes, Lord," she whispered.

"I see. Then if you are here as a sort of high priestess supposed to be worshipping me, why did you stick your tongue out at me?"

She was silent again and then suddenly looked up at

him defiantly, though there were tears in her eyes.

"Because I was bored," she said. "Now kill me, Lord."

And she held her arms out wide as though presenting herself to him as a sacrifice.

He closed his eyes at the beauty of her and turned away again.

"Don't be a silly little fool," he said gruffly. "I wouldn't dream of killing you."

"The Lord means it?"

"Of course I do."

"The Lord's humble servant is grateful."

"Look, forget about this humble servant and Lord business, will you? I'm not a Lord and you're not a humble servant—"

"But now that the Lord is awake after all this time I wish to be his humble servant."

"Hm. I'm not sure that that would be a good thing. Listen, Selena, how long have I been asleep?"

"I don't know, Lord. The elders say it has been a long, long time."

"I can appreciate that. But why the temple?"

"Because the Lord is the Lord."

"That doesn't mean anything, Selena. Besides, I'm not a god. I'm just a person like you."

(And why had he said that when he knew it wasn't true?)

"Oh, surely not, Lord," she said.

"Yes."

"I don't think so," she said seriously. "The Lord is different. He does not have these."

And she touched her breasts which bobbed enchantingly.

"No, well, perhaps not—"

"And the Lord is different here as well—"

"Yes, yes, I know. I mean I'm the same kind of person as you—Oh, forget it. Just tell me why the temple is here. Pretend that I'm a complete stranger who knows nothing about you whatsoever, and you have to explain to me from the very beginning."

She was frowning in some confusion.

"What is a stranger?" she asked.

"Someone from far away that you have never seen before."

"A baby?"

"No. A grown person."

She shook her head in puzzlement.

"I do not understand this," she said. "How could there be a grown person whom I do not know?"

No strangers . . . A closed society. His mind clicked a notch and registered the fact.

"Never mind," he said slowly. "We'll talk about that later. Just tell me the story of *me* and the temple."

"But that's silly. The Lord knows it already."

"Well, pretend the Lord's had a bump on the head and lost his memory, and you've got to remind him."

She looked at him with concern, reached out a hand to touch him and then thought better of it.

"Has that happened to the Lord?"

"Yes, it has."

"I am sorry. If it will help him to recover his memory I will tell him the story. This is the Lord's temple, and we watch over him waiting for the day when he will awaken, because on that day he will arise and help us to solve all our problems."

"You have problems?"

"Yes, Lord. We have problems. I have problems, too," she whispered, and glanced up at him through her thick eyelashes.

He swallowed and shifted a little further away from her on the catafalque. Really, it was very difficult to concentrate.

"Where is my ship?" he asked.

"Ship?"

He looked at her.

"You don't know?"

She shook her head, her eyes wide.

"No, Lord. I don't know what a ship is."

"Selena, there is a lot I have to learn about you. And there is a lot you have to learn about me."

"The Lord does me much honor."

"The Lord finds you terribly distracting."

"I must summon the elders. There will be trouble if I delay," she said and she jumped off the catafalque.

Trist grabbed her hand as she passed him and she stopped obediently.

"What will happen when you summon the elders? he asked.

"They will come with ceremonies and take the Lord away from the temple to help them solve their problems."

"I see. And you? What will happen to you?"

"I don't know. Maybe there will be no more temple duties now the Lord is awake," she said, and she seemed pleasantly diverted at the thought.

"Will I see you again?"

"Of course. Whenever the Lord wishes."

"I'm glad."

He drew her gently to him. She came willingly at first, and then as his head came down to hers she suddenly resisted. But his arms were round the warm smoothness of her naked waist and he found himself trembling with a desire such as he had never experienced before.

"No, Lord, no—" she whispered.

Her lips were soft and yielding and he felt her quiver for a moment as though he had roused in her a passion similar to his own, and then far too soon she broke away from him, trying to free herself from the grip of his arms.

"No," she gasped. "This is bad. The Lord must not—"

"Why not—?" he asked, holding her.

She pushed down on his arms with her hands, and although he could easily have held her had he wanted to, he had no wish to force her against her will, and he reluctantly released her.

"The Lord shouldn't. Really, he shouldn't," she murmured, her face suddenly gravely concerned. "He makes things difficult—"

"Just to kiss you—"

"This is bad, Lord. Now I must summon the elders."

She turned and walked away towards a corner of the temple, and he followed the graceful movement of her body with a desire suddenly gone cold.

She reached up to a cord which hung from one of the many draperies in the temple and pulled it.

Muffled and distant he heard the ringing of a bell.

Trist sat on the catafalque and gazed at the patterned rugs on the floor of the temple. That way he was not distracted by the sight of her and he could concentrate on questions which were bothering him.

How did she know his language? Where was he? Where was his ship? If he had lost that he might as well abandon the search for corenium here and now. And why had Selena drawn away from him like that? Well, maybe he would find some of the answers when the elders, whoever they might be, arrived at the temple.

3

Selena's phrase about the elders coming with ceremonies had conjured up a picture of solemn music and a dignified procession bearing strange banners. The reality was so different as to be almost farcical.

The double doors at the end of the temple opened a

125

fraction and a head poked through. It looked round, caught sight of him standing by the catafalque, gasped in amazement and hastily withdrew. But it forgot to close the door properly, and it swung slowly and silently open, giving a view of a wide corridor beyond. Just outside the doors a group of elderly people were talking in hurried whispers and jostling and pushing themselves into some sort of order. Suddenly one of them noticed that the door was open, drew the attention of the others to it, and all of them tried to straighten up and assume a kind of dignity which had been totally lacking ten seconds before.

Trist found it hard not to smile. But, he thought, Selena had told him he was a god and this was his temple. He had not the slightest idea of the way a god should behave, and he could not obtain respect by magical use of his technology as he had done with the Picts so long ago. For one thing, these people were not savages to be impressed by magic, and for another, with no ship he had almost no technology.

An attitude of distant dignity would be best until he was given some clue to what was expected of him.

He came to the edge of the steps leading down from the catafalque to the floor of the temple and waited. The deputation had formed up in some kind of order and was now advancing steadily towards him.

He counted five men and four women, all of them middle-aged to elderly, each wearing a kind of loose white garment, the women's hanging from both shoulders, the men's from one, all of them reaching to their ankles. Most of them had grey hair, some snow white, and their faces were lined with wrinkles which he thought were of experience rather than suffering. There was a calm dignity about them which he found impressive.

They stopped before they reached the steps and bowed. It was a ragged movement, done with no kind
126

of precision, rather as though it were a spontaneous gesture than one connected with ceremonial and carefully rehearsed. From this position at the top of the steps to the catafalque they seemed very fragile creatures.

Trist raised a hand.

"Greetings," he said solemnly.

Out of the corner of his eye he saw Selena stealing along the wall of the temple, heading for the door which still stood open. He wanted to call to her to wait, but he thought better of it. She had said he could see her again whenever he wished.

One of the men stepped forward. He was perhaps the oldest of them all, but he held himself well. His face was pale but serene and kindly and his faded blue eyes were respectful. His hands were thin and well-kept and the blue veins stood out clearly.

"We welcome you, Lord," he said. "We are at your service."

And he lowered his head again.

Trist could not resist it.

"Was it you who stuck his head through the door just now?" he asked.

The man nodded.

"Yes, Lord," he said contritely. "Forgive the unseemliness of my behaviour. We have waited so long for you to awaken that when it happened at last we found it hard to believe."

"What is your name?"

"The Lord does me much honour. I am Fardon, Lord, the Chief Elder."

He turned and introduced each member of the deputation by name, but Trist found it impossible to remember them all. Each one bowed respectfully as his or her name was mentioned, and then Fardon turned back.

"The ceremonial welcome will by now be arranged,"

he said. "Would it please the Lord to attend the festivity in his honour?"

"It would please me," said Trist with a straight face.

Though I'd much rather relieve myself, have a quick bath and then see Selena again, he thought. Why had she broken away from his kiss . . . ?

The deputation turned and split into two groups, one on each side of the aisle to the door. Trist took the hint and strode down the steps to ground level. The elders formed up on either side of him so that he was surrounded by a ceremonial guard and they marched slowly and solemnly to the temple door and out. Even on the same level he was head and shoulders taller than the tallest of them.

Beyond the door was a long, wide corridor which was empty. The procession made its way along this corridor, and Trist noticed doors set into the dull grey walls at intervals on either side, but there was no sign of any people. Some of the doors were open and he managed to glimpse occasional work benches in the rooms beyond, and it seemed that in places fairly complicated and technical processes were going on, but there was no one actively engaged in work. It was as if the people suddenly left what they were doing to attend some more important function.

Like a ceremony of welcome, he thought as he became aware of a murmur of sound somewhere ahead.

His mind recognized something which had been nagging at him since they had left the temple. The corridor was lit artificially and there were no windows in any of the rooms he had glimpsed.

"When do we get outside?" he asked casually.

Fardon, who was walking at his right side, turned to him respectfully.

"We are now outside the precincts of the temple, Lord," he said.

Trist nodded as though he were satisfied with the

explanation, but his mind was beginning to slip into a faster rhythm.

They were underground. Or at least, they were in an environment which was closed to the outside air. And he gathered that the word "Outside" did not have quite the same meaning to Fardon as it had for him.

That was logical thought, but then he realized that Fardon and he were speaking the same language, and everything seemed to whirl away into meaninglessness again.

The corridor suddenly debauched into a large amphitheater, and the procession wheeled left and mounted a short flight of steps to a platform.

There they turned and faced the amphitheater.

It was a circular expanse with corridors leading off it at regular intervals, but again there was no view of the outside world, only the same even glow lighting the drab grey metallic-looking walls which he had noticed in the corridor.

The amphitheater was crowded with people. At a rough guess there were about five hundred of them. They wore simple tunics, most of them considerably shorter than the staid-looking robes of the elders, and of brighter and more varied colours.

The elders spread out along the edge of the platform where a metal rail cut off the drop to the ground below, leaving the center of the platform for Trist. He stood with his hands on the rail and looked down at the crowd. Every one of them was staring at him, eyes wide with awe and interest. There were children and adults of all shapes, sizes and types, and yet looking at them, Trist had the curious feeling that there was a monotonous similarity about them which he found hard to pinpoint. It was a lack of character, a total difference from what he had been so attracted to in Selena.

One of the elders stepped forward and began to

129

speak, and Trist tried to concentrate on what was being said. It was a long, rambling speech, and Trist found it hard enough to follow the strange accent and the unusual words without having to contend with the man's poor diction as well, but he managed to pick out the salient points.

"... Give thanks for your return ... help us to a better, fuller life ... save us from the burning heat ... from monsters and the wasting death ... bring us to the light ... let the bells ring to show us the way ... keep us whole and in our right minds ... deliver us from the burning heat ... let not the monsters walk among us ..."

It went on rather like an incantation, and through it all the prayer for preservation from the burning heat and for the warding off of monsters was repeated again and again.

His mind slipped back ... He heard again the alarm which had emptied the streets of the Town Complex and he remembered the fear which he had found in the people he encountered. Prudence Briggs had murmured deliriously about hydrogen and cobalt bombs just before she died. She had told him to get to one of the shelters ...

The world had been on the brink of nuclear war.

With the precision of a computer, elements began to fall into place. This was an immense underground shelter. Not long after Prudence Briggs's time a nuclear attack had taken place and a group had sheltered here. This would explain the constant references to the burning heat and the vital necessity for keeping it out of the closed environment. It explained why Selena had not understood what a stranger was. In a closed environment such as this no one would be a stranger. You could never meet someone you had never met before. The concept of a strange adult did not exist.

It would also explain the need to ward off monsters.

130

If mutations appeared the true strain might die out . . .

The voice of the elder droned on as Trist assembled these facts. There were gaps still, but they could be filled in later. He was sure that basically he was right, though there were aspects of his theory which did not quite hold together.

And how had he got here, anyway?

Excavations for the nuclear shelters might have uncovered the ship. Having discovered it he could imagine the sequence of events. They would break into it, find him not dead but in a state of suspended animation and remove him and take him into the shelter with them. The circumstances of his discovery would be so bizarre that it might suggest to them that if they were incarcerated in a nuclear shelter and he woke up, his advanced technology might help them to recover what they had lost. He would be an insurance for the future. And until he woke up, he would consume none of their food, drink none of their water, breathe none of their air. He would cost them nothing and he might repay them a lot.

This would explain their belief now that he was some kind of a god. During goodness knew how many generations the fact that he must be preserved pending recovery so that he could help them would become part of the pattern of their lives.

How long had it been? If his previous length of sleep was anything to go by it must be about fifteen hundred of this planet's years. So it was natural that the people should have forgotten what the outside world was like. He remembered Fardon's ignorance of what "Outside" meant. They would be left with a memory of a better life, one which they did not know from experience but which they would constantly recall in stories and symbols, and his own presence would be a tangible reminder of their need for help to return to better things.

131

The only point which didn't fit was why they had never found their way back to the surface themselves. Surely the effect of radiation would not have lasted so long that they could have completely forgotten about the life they had left behind? And yet it seemed as if it must have done.

Trist came back to the present with a start to realize that the elder had finished speaking and that the crowd was gazing at him wonderingly, waiting for him to say something.

He knew he should bring forth some resounding phrase which would impress them deeply and convince them of his god-like status, but all he was conscious of was his overwhelming need to relieve himself. He would have to get away from this ceremony fairly soon or there would be a most ungod-like accident.

He raised his hand in what he hoped was an impressive gesture.

"Greetings," he said solemnly. "My name is Trist. I came from far away many, many years ago. I hope I may be able to help you with your problems, and later I shall confer with your elders as to the exact nature of the problems you have. But in the meantime I am hungry and tired—" and desperate, he thought, "—and would like to rest for a while before we discuss these things."

He stepped back from the rail to show he had finished and the crowd murmured and jostled slightly, but they seemed satisfied with what he had said. Trist turned to Fardon.

"Is there somewhere where I can be alone for a while?" he asked.

Fardon bowed his head.

"Yes, Lord. There has always been an apartment laid aside for your use whenever you should arise to claim it. I shall show you where it is."

The procession formed up round him and marched

132

down the steps at the end of the platform and into the corridor again. As far as Trist could tell they seemed to be returning to the temple, but the procession stopped before they reached it and Fardon gestured towards a door.

"This is your apartment, Lord," he said.

"Thank you," said Trist. He strode to the door which one of the other elders hurried to open for him. Beyond, he could see a small vestibule with several doors opening off it. One must be the room he needed, he thought. But he could scarcely bolt into the place unceremoniously, and there was something he wanted to make sure of before he cut himself off temporarily from these people.

"The girl who was in the temple when I awoke," he began.

Fardon turned to one of the female elders and she whispered something to him.

"Selena," he said.

"Yes. Selena. I should like to see her if it is convenient."

Fardon bowed, accepting the request with neither surprise nor protest.

"She will be sent to you, Lord," he said.

"Thank you," said Trist. "I shall see you all again soon."

They bowed and he bowed back and stepped inside the apartment, closing the door behind him. With an enormous sense of urgency he hurried to find the room he needed.

4

Trist sat back on the deep couch which had moulded itself to his shape. The soft lighting and rich drapery which hid the metal walls was very soothing. He had found the bathroom and done what was needful and had also had a bath. Stripping off his space suit had been a joy, and the soft touch of warm water and jets of scented soap had taken the stiffness out of muscles which had grown used to lying in the same position. He had found a long tunic such as the elders wore hanging in the main room and he had put it on, revelling in its lightness and comfort, even though it was very much shorter on him than it was meant to be. He had also found a cart laden with delicacies which he had sampled ravenously and found edible, but curiously lacking in taste and texture. The reconstituted food and drink on the *Revelation* had tasted better than this. He could almost hear the roar of fury from Captain Graud if the taste of the food fell below his own strict standards.

Now he lay relaxed, looking at the ceiling of the room, wondering how much solid earth and rock lay between it and the surface of the planet.

He tried to analyse his attitude of mind. He had lost his ship, he was almost certain there would be no corenium here anyway, and he must now be many thousands of years beyond the time he had known in Haven. Yet this did not worry him. He felt uneasy and claustrophobic, lying here knowing that he was surrounded on all sides by earth, far from the open air. He wondered at this feeling. It seemed paradoxical for a space man who spent large periods of life cooped up in a closed environment far tighter than this, but he realised that at least he had a view of the grandeur of infinity out of the viewports. Here there was nothing, and it was grossly unnatural.

Even this, however, did not detract from the feeling of contentment which had crept over him. In this alien and unnatural atmosphere he had for some reason found peace.

The door slid open and his thoughts crystalized. This

was his peace and contentment. This was the focal point of his life.

She came quietly into the room and the door slid shut behind her.

She was wearing a simple white tunic with a narrow yellow belt at her waist, and a pair of white sandals on her feet. Her hair was drawn back and tied with a yellow ribbon. She stood with her hands clasped in front of her, her eyes on the floor.

"The Lord sent for me," she said quietly.

He stood up and came towards her, taking her hands gently in his.

"I *asked* if you would come," he said.

She looked up at him briefly from under her lashes and then looked away again.

"It was an order."

"No. It was a request."

"Therefore I came."

"Selena, you mustn't think of it that way. If I ask you to do something, then you must only do it if you want to, not because you have been told to. Do you understand that?"

"Yes, Lord."

"And please don't keep calling me Lord."

He led her to the couch and she sat down, and clasped her hands demurely round her knees.

"My name is Trist. Please won't you call me by my name?"

"Yes, Lord Trist."

In her mouth the blunt monosyllable seemed suddenly to have caught a beautiful music he had not been aware of before. He sat in a rosy glow of wonder as he looked at her profile, at the gentle tilt of her nose, at the long lashes and the small, determined chin.

"I'm glad you came, Selena."

"I am glad the Lord sent for—asked me," she said.

"Why?"

135

She flushed and refused to meet his eye.

"In the temple—just before I summoned the elders," she said hesitantly. "The Lord did something —something he shouldn't have done—"

"I kissed you."

"Yes. He kissed me. That was it. Please—would the Lord do that again?"

And suddenly she turned to him a little fearfully, her eyes wide, her mouth slightly open, and Trist restrained himself with an effort.

"Last time you didn't seem to want me to," he said.

"I know. It is bad and wrong. But I liked it, Lord. For all that the elders say, I don't believe that something you like is wrong."

"There is nothing wrong with kissing," said Trist, and he put his hands on her shoulders and drew her gently to him.

Her mouth was soft and warm on his, and this time there was an eagerness and an abandonment there had not been before. Her body hardened against his, and he held her gently, mindful of his unaccustomed strength, willing himself not to hurt her, though his instinct was to crush her to him.

He lost count of time, and indeed it might have stopped altogether, but at last she drew away with a little moan.

"Oh, the Lord is good to me," she murmured.

Her tunic had ridden up over the sweet curve of her thighs, and he put his hand under it and tried to ease it upwards, but she drew away.

"What is it, Lord?" she asked.

"I want you, Selena—" he said hoarsely.

She smoothed her tunic down hastily.

"I don't understand this," she said, and her face looked a little lost. "In the temple the Lord wanted me dressed. Now that I am dressed the Lord wants to take it off. What is the reason for this?"

He was taken aback by the question because he would never have thought it needed to be asked.

"Because I love you, Selena, and I want to have you," he said with absolute truth.

She seemed suddenly to understand what he meant and she moved further down the couch, shaking her head, her eyes full of fear.

"No," she whispered. "No. You mustn't, Lord. That's wrong. Very wrong."

He was puzzled. He knew she needed him. He was sure she was attracted to him. For the first time she had addressed him directly instead of in the third person. Why this sudden barrier?

"I see the Lord is not aware of our ways," she said solemnly. "I'm sorry I should have realized the Lord is different from us."

"Selena, what is it that frightens you?"

"Physical contact is highly dangerous," she intoned as though she were reciting some long-remembered lesson.

Mutations, he thought. The fear of mutations in the closed circuit of this existence. A terrible danger . . .

"You have children here?" he asked.

"Oh, yes, Lord."

"Where do they come from?"

"From the test tubes, of course."

He let out his breath in a sigh of understanding.

"Artificial babies," he murmured, more to himself than to her.

"No, Lord. Pure babies."

All right, he thought. That was a question of semantics. He could understand the need to reproduce artificially in order to avoid the possibility of mutation, but there were problems in avoiding ordinary births.

"Do you know about sex?" he asked.

She nodded.

"Yes, Lord. We are taught the dangers of it very

137

early, and we are given drugs to help us to avoid it."

Kill the sex urge, he thought. That way you avoided the possibility of accidents. All births channelled through laboratory test tubes. He looked at her and found it impossible to believe. She could never have come out of a test tube. Nothing so warm and vibrant and alive could have been born of sterility. His heart cried out at the enormity of the idea.

And then he suddenly recalled something.

"But it doesn't always work, does it?" he said.

She blushed and looked away.

"No, Lord," she muttered.

"Selena, what is a Natural?"

"Lord, please—"

"You're a Natural, aren't you, Selena?"

"Yes, Lord, but it's not my fault—"

"Accidents happen, is that it? Sometimes the drugs don't work, or nature reasserts itself and two people mate and produce a natural child."

Tears came running down her cheeks now and her head was hanging in shame.

"The Lord is unkind," she sobbed.

He seized her shoulders and shook her gently.

"Don't be a silly fool," he said, his heart singing again. "I'm glad! You're a Natural. I'm a Natural too. Don't you see—it's the biggest compliment anyone could pay you, to call you a Natural. You're a real person—not a machine—made automaton.

"I have never been ashamed of it before—"

"Then don't start now. Tell me about the Naturals."

"Must I Lord?"

"Yes. Please, Selena."

She took a deep breath and clasped her hands tightly together as though she were facing some ordeal.

"They keep examining us to make sure we are not monsters," she said. "I don't think I'm a monster, and I don't want to be one, but they say I might be without

138

knowing it. We are put on temple duty instead of training for other work because they think that the sin which caused our birth might be handed on to us, and temple duty is a way of thinking purifying thoughts and purging ourselves of the bad things the drugs are supposed to take away. Though what we will do now that you have awakened, Lord, I don't know. We can live the same lives as the others, but they watch us all the time . . ."

"And what happened to your parents?"

"Parents?"

"The people who gave you birth."

"Oh. They are operated on so that it can't happen again."

"When do they give you these drugs?"

"When these begin to grow, Lord," she cupped her breasts under her tunic, "and when we grow hair here and down here."

"How effective do you think these drugs are?"

"Oh, they are good, Lord. I—I'm sure they're good."

"But they haven't worked on you, have they?"

She stared at him, eyes wide in horror, mouth open.

"Oh, yes, Lord! They have, they have! They must have—!"

"Selena, they haven't, or you wouldn't have wanted me to kiss you just now."

She buried her face in her hands and sobbed wildly.

"Oh, please—it's just that—the Lord is so good and—and comforting—and—and I'm lonely—I want —I don't know what I want—Oh, Lord, help me, Please!"

He took her hands again and gently kissed her wet eyes and held her to him while the trembling lessened and the sobbing eased.

"Tell me, Selena," he said at last. "Has any Natural ever proved to be a monster?"

"I don't think so, Lord."

"So, really, there's no danger in people mating, is there?"

"Oh, yes, Lord. It's bad and evil—"

"Selena, it's nothing of the sort. You've been told that for so long you half believe it, but your instincts are rebelling. Selena, will you trust me?"

She looked at him and sniffed.

"Yes, Lord," she said.

"Will you believe that I want to show you what life is really all about? That what we do is not wrong, and that without this, life has no point at all?"

She was frowning slightly.

"What do you want to do to me, Lord?" she asked.

"I'll show you. But promise me one thing. Don't stop because you think it may be wrong. Only stop if you don't like it. All right?"

She nodded, and he took her into his arms.

Carefully, he thought. Be very gentle. Be patient.

It was easier said than done. She was so beautiful and there was such an air of innocence about her that he was deeply moved. He set about allaying her fears, speaking softly and tenderly to her, stroking her hair until she began to relax at the comforting sound of his voice.

And gradually he felt desire take over from her fear. The deep unconquerable instincts began to dominate. Without protest she allowed him to unfasten her tunic and throw it aside, and in response she pulled his own robe off his shoulder and he felt it drop round his ankles.

That was his last coherent thought. Suddenly the claustrophobic walls and ceiling fell away and they were floating on clouds of brightness with the sun caressing their naked bodies, twining and fusing into one as they climbed higher and higher on the path to an unbelievable glory. Haven and corenium and Captain

Graud and the scout ship were totally unimportant. They were alone together and nothing else mattered, and as they reached a perfect climax the three thousand years of loneliness fell away as though they had never been, and he had come safely home at last.

5

He lay on the couch, drained and incredibly happy, Selena warm in his arms, her head on his chest and her dark hair tickling his nose. She was very still and he thought she was asleep.

All right, maybe the underground complex was not an ideal environment, but so long as she was with him he could be contented with it. He knew that this could be a reaction to the loss of his home, his people and his identity, a straw which the drowning man clutched at as being the first and only means of support. But while there was some truth in that it was not the whole truth. Selena was more than a straw.

He shifted his head slightly so that he could look down at her, at the curving length of her naked body which he knew so well now. He wanted nothing more than to continue to know and explore and delight in its magical beauty for the rest of his days. Her face was hidden from him, turned away and masked by her hair, and he stroked the hair aside so that he could see her better.

She turned further away, but not quickly enough, and he saw the glitter of tears in her eyes. He sat up slowly, drawing her up with him, his deep contentment evaporating suddenly. She was crying slightly and bitterly as though her heart was breaking.

"What is it my darling?" he asked softly.

It seemed to release a dam. She leant forward with her head on his shoulder and sobbed loudly and hopelessly while he could do nothing but stroke his

141

hand up and down her spine and murmur endearments. At last she seemed to drain herself dry and was silent except for an occasional shuddering sniff.

Then he made her lift her head from his shoulder and he sat looking into the shimmering pools of her eyes.

"Did I hurt you?" he asked.

She nodded miserably.

"Yes, Lord," she said. "The Lord is so big. It was sore to begin with but I did not mind that. It—it was so beautiful, Lord I—I didn't know there was such beauty and happiness. I think—that was what I have been looking for for a long, long time."

"Then what is troubling you?"

"I am sorry because it can't happen again."

"Why shouldn't it?"

"The elders will find out. And they will operate on me. And on you. And they will give us drugs. They will make the Lord unfit to enter me and I will never know the joy of feeling the Lord inside me again. What we have done is forbidden, Lord, though now I don't understand why."

She looked at him imploringly and his need for her began to swell again, but there were important issues here which had to be dealt with first.

He stood up and picked up her tunic from the floor and handed it to her.

"Put that on, my darling, before I get diverted again," he said.

"The Lord does not find me pleasing any more?" she asked, her voice a little hurt.

"The Lord finds you too pleasing," he said. "The Lord can't think when you stand in front of him like that."

A little puzzled, she pulled the tunic on over her head.

"That's better," he said as it settled round her body

and she tightened the belt at her waist. "Now listen. Are there any maps of this place?"

"Maps, Lord?"

"Yes. Maps. Ground plans. Diagrams." Her face remained blank. "Pictures of what this place looks like."

Her face cleared.

"Oh, pictures of the world," she said "Yes, Lord."

"Can you get some?"

"Yes, Lord."

"Then do that and bring them back here as quickly as you can."

She nodded and ran towards the door.

"Selena," he called after her, and she stopped. "The elders—are they really likely to find out soon?"

Her face clouded over again.

"I had forgotten," she said quietly. "Yes. They will. I did not tell the Lord before, but I have an examination today."

"Today?"

"Yes, Lord. They examine the Naturals during every seventh twenty-four hour period. This is the seventh."

He frowned.

"I wish you'd told me that before," he said.

"The Lord made me forget," she said with gentle accusation, and he knew that he would have forgotten himself in any case, and the knowledge would probably not have stopped him.

"What will happen?" he asked.

"When they find that I am no longer as I was before they will order the operation. They will probably increase the drugs, too." Suddenly she looked lost and woebegone. "And then we shall never be able to do it again, Lord."

"We shall," he said confidently. "Don't worry. But only if you get those pictures."

She nodded, ran back to him and kissed him, and

143

then hurried to the door and went out.

Trist let out a deep sigh and sat down on the couch, staring unseeingly at the drapes hanging on the wall opposite him. Quite deliberately he set himself to the questions facing him and their possible solutions.

To begin with, the people in this environment regarded him as a god who would help solve their problems. But he had already been forced to pose unsuccessfully as a god for the Picts. Here there were customs which appeared inflexible and which he had already broken, and if his transgression was discovered, as seemed inevitable, no amount of godhood would save him from an undesirable penalty.

Therefore he must avoid that penalty, and there were only two ways of doing that. He could escape from the environment and leave them to carry on as they had done for many hundreds of years. But that would mean either leaving Selena behind or taking her with him. The former was unthinkable, the latter might be impossible. Or he could stay and try to convince the elders that their reasoning was all wrong and that they should change their laws. That, he felt, might take more persuasion than even a god could manage.

There was another possibility which was really a combination of the two, and it all depended on one thing. There were several clues which made him think the possibility might prove practical . . .

Selena.

Whatever happened he must make sure that she was safe. For a moment he was able to stand outside himself and see how ridiculous the situation was. He had travelled he did not know how many millions of millions of miles, spent he did not know how long in suspended animation, and then suddenly found his whole life centered around an alien girl whose intelligence was sharp but whose knowledge was limited by the walls of a subterranean nuclear shelter.

144

By all the laws of nature it couldn't have happened. It was ethically wrong and biologically impossible. He from Haven, she from this planet. The odds against two species finding such compatibility must be enormous, and yet it had happened.

The experience which he and Selena had shared had been so basic, so unutterably beautiful and so *right* that there must be something . . .

An idea was beginning to grow in his mind. It was ludicrous but insistent, and there was a fundamental grain of logic in it which he knew he had to examine . . .

When Selena returned, she found him sitting, staring at the wall, his mind far away, grappling with problems which had suddenly risen in unexpected places, and he was unaware of her presence until she timidly touched his shoulder.

Then he returned with a start and looked at her slim loveliness.

He loved her. He knew that.

He could not love an alien. He knew that.

Therefore she was not alien. And instinctively he knew this to be a fact.

And then the questions began . . .

No matter. There might be time for answers later. But now there was work to be done.

"I have brought the picture, Lord," she said. "Did I do right?"

"Yes, Selena. You did right. Why do you ask?"

"The Lord seemed so solemn when I came in. I thought he might not like to be disturbed."

He took the sheet she held out to him and squeezed her hand gently.

"You disturb me all the time," he said. "And I'm glad."

He spread the plan out on the table by the couch and she knelt beside him as he looked at it.

The shelter complex was wheel-shaped with the central amphitheater as the hub. From the hub corridors sprang like spokes. Rings cut the spokes at intervals to form cross corridors so that people wishing to get from one corridor to another did not always have to go to the amphitheater first. But there was no rim to the wheel. The spoke corridors ended in blankness, as though there had been an intention to extend them further had time permitted the builders to do so. But there were four corridors, one in each quarter of the wheel, which ended in a red barrier, and Trist guessed these must be the exits, long forgotten and forbidden to the people.

He located the temple by its shape and found that the corridor on which it stood had an exit at the end of it.

Now he knew what he had to do.

"Selena," he said. "I'm going outside."

She looked at him enquiringly.

"To the corridor, Lord?" she asked.

"Further than that. Right outside. Outside this whole area."

He tapped the map and suddenly she seemed to realize what he meant and fear started into her eyes.

"Oh, no, Lord!" she said. "You mustn't! There is nothing Outside except the burning heat. It is death to go Outside!"

"So your elders keep telling you, but I'm not quite so sure."

"The bells will ring when it is safe to open the doors."

"Yes, I've heard about those bells. Well, maybe they've short-circuited or something. Anyway, someone's got to go out there and see what's going on."

"No, Lord, no! No one has ever returned from Outside!"

He looked at her sharply.

146

"You mean people have tried?" he asked.

She gulped and nodded.

"Yes, Lord," she said. "But no one has tried for a long, long time. The last was a girl called Jennifox. She was a Natural, like me. She was mentally unbalanced, the elders say, and she left a note saying where she was going."

"How did she get out?"

"I don't know, Lord. She never came back. The burning heat took her. If it happened to Jennifox, it will happen to the Lord too. Oh, please, Lord, don't go! For my sake, don't go!"

"I must, Selena. And I'm sure there's no danger."

"There is. Please!" She gulped, and then went on with a curious and moving dignity. "If anything happens to the Lord I shall die. When you looked at me for the first time in the temple, Lord, I felt excited and happy and afraid all at once. You make me feel things I have never felt before. There is a tenderness in my heart for you, Lord Trist. It is presumptuous of me to say so, but it is the truth, and if you go and don't return I shall have no reason to go on living."

He drew her to him.

"My darling, that's the nicest thing anyone has ever said to me without using the word love," he said.

"I do not understand love."

"You understand it very well, although you may never have come across the word before. But I'm not going to die, Selena. I have my suit. So even if there is burning heat outside, my suit will keep me safe until I find out. Then I shall return and tell you whether it is safe now to go out or not."

He took her to the couch and began to speak to her about Outside. About the trees and fields he had known earlier, both on this world and on his own, about the sky and the distant stars and the brightness of the sun, and the softness of the rain and the wind, and she

147

stared at him, only half comprehending what he was saying but fascinated by the pictures he drew. He knew it was possible that outside now there was a barren desert of ashes and emptiness, but he wanted her to know only of the pleasant things. He told her finally of the marvellous satellite which this planet had and how in the darkness it glowed and shed a soft light, and how it waxed and waned and was called the moon. She seemed fascinated by the moon.

"It must be very beautiful," she said a little wistfully.

"It is," he said. "Thousands of years ago an ancient people of this planet gave a name to the moon. They called it Selene. Somehow that name has survived in you."

She was intrigued, but he knew it was little more than a fairy tale to her. It was necessary that she should know, though, because soon the outside world would become a reality—he hoped. And if it did she must be prepared for it.

6

Trist held Selena's hand and looked at the wall which blocked his way to freedom.

"There, Lord, you see," she said, and there was thankfulness in her voice. "There is no way to Outside."

The map of the underground complex had been deceptive, for there was no scale marked on it. They must have walked for more than twenty minutes before they eventually left the last of the cross corridors behind and stepped into what he knew instinctively was an uninhabited area. They had met few people during their walk, and those had stood aside with heads bowed humbly, and he had raised his hand regally to them in a gesture which he hoped conveyed power and com-passion and confidence all at the same time.

Behind them the corridor had taken a slight turn to the left and the view back was cut off. What Selena had said seemed true. There was no way through this barrier. No sign of hinges, no handles, no bolts, no locking mechanism, nothing.

He stepped forward and examined the surface minutely, feeling Selena step close behind him, not wanting him to get too far away, not wanting him to leave her and go into the terrible burning heat.

On a level with his waist he detected a hairline crack on the smooth surface of the wall.

"Here we are," he breathed. "Look at that."

His finger traced the outline of a circle large enough for a man to get through.

But a man of his size . . . ? It would be a tight squeeze, but he was sure he could manage it.

"That's it," he said. "Not large enough to get in all the equipment which must have been brought in here. It must be a wicket gate . . . Yes. The whole wall must move. But how do we open this?"

"It is not meant that we should try to open it," said Selena hopefully.

"It is not meant that you should spend your life cooped up here when it may not be necessary," he said, and he stepped back and examined the walls and ceiling of the corridor near the end barrier, while Selena stood uncertainly, twining her fingers together, watching him with fearful eyes.

Suddenly he grunted.

"Got it," he said, and pointed. She followed his hand and saw high on the curving wall of the corridor a small metal door with a recessed handle.

"Even I can't reach that," he said. "Selena. You'll have to try it."

For a moment she looked rebellious, but a glance at his face must have convinced her that rebellion would do no good.

149

"What must I do, Lord?" she asked.

"I'll lift you on to my shoulders and you will have to open that door and see what's inside."

"Please, Lord, must we do this?"

"Yes, we must. Come on, now."

He knelt on the ground and under his instructions she stepped on to his shoulders, using the wall to steady herself with her hands. Then very slowly he stood up again and she adjusted her balance with one hand on the wall until she was standing upright on his shoulders. Her weight seemed very slight and he could barely feel the pressure of her sandalled feet through the material of his suit. He stood quite still, facing the barrier at the end of the corridor and listened to the heavy breathing above him.

"The little door is open, Lord," she said at last.

"Good. What's inside?"

"There is a kind of handle."

"Right. Pull it."

She grunted and he could feel her weight shift slightly on his shoulders.

"It is very—stiff, Lord. I—I don't think—I can manage it—"

And then suddenly the handle must have moved, for she staggered. He caught her as she fell, and the firm softness of her was in his arms again and her warm mouth was working on his. He felt her press herself to him, but the suit was a barrier and the place too public and after a moment with deep regret he pushed her gently away.

"Don't go, Lord," she whispered. "Please."

"I must," he said. "Look."

She turned as he nodded his head towards the barrier. The round circle was more pronounced now, and when they approached it Trist found that it had sprung back a little and he could ease his fingers through the gap. The circular part turned slightly. He

150

pushed it round and it unthreaded a screw. And how had Jennifox managed that alone? he wondered. With a ladder which she had taken the trouble to replace or hide before she went out trembling to whatever faced her beyond? He turned back to Selena.

"You must not stay here now," he said. "Go back to the apartment and stay there until I return. Will you do that?"

"If the Lord is going to be burned by the heat I want to be burned by it too."

"I'm not going to be burned by it. The suit will protect me. But if you come with me now you might be burned for you have no suit, and I don't want that to happen."

"You will come back, Lord? Truly?"

"Truly, Selena."

She nodded slowly and reluctantly.

"Then I will wait in the Lord's apartment. Be careful, Lord."

He kissed her and then switched on his oxygen supply and closed the face-plate of his helmet. He turned quickly and rotated the circular door until it came loose and folded downwards. When he looked back Selena had disappeared.

With some difficulty he eased himself through the opening and flicked on his helmet lamp, for it was dark here. He replaced the circular opening and screwed it tight, noting that there was a handle on this side to open it again. Then he walked to the far end of the little cell he found himself in.

An air lock, he thought, turning his head this way and that so that the beam on his helmet lamp flickered round the walls.

It was a gigantic double door, massive and heavy looking, and it gave the impression of being very thick. The doors were bolted tight, but steady pressure on the bolts released them and they fell apart.

He pushed one of the doors and it swung easily open a fraction. He paused and looked at his wrist geiger. The needle had scarcely moved.

He pushed the door further open and walked through.

The tunnel beyond was hewn out of the rock. Its walls and floor were rough and uneven, and it sloped gently upwards as far as the beam of his lamp would show.

He must not delay, for there could be very little oxygen left in his suit pack . . .

As he strode upwards along the rough tunnel his mind was turning over the facts. Anyone could have got out of the underground complex if they had wanted to, but the fear of radiation had been so deeply instilled in them that escape must have been the last thing they would contemplate—except for occasional people like Jennifox who, for some reason, perhaps claustrophobia, had found shelter life intolerable and had been prepared to risk the burning heat to get away. He could imagine, all those years ago, the alarm shrilling as it had shrilled when he and Prudence Briggs had escaped from the Productivity Department Building. He remembered how the streets had emptied so suddenly and how, even as she was dying, she had murmured about the bombs and the need to find shelter.

And some time after that it had not been a false alarm. The people had run to the shelters when the bells sounded, shut themselves in and waited. Only that time there had been no one left to set off the all clear, telling them that they could re-emerge. So they had settled and waited. Waited and waited. They must have been prepared to wait many years if there really had been an attack.

The years had passed and the bells had never rung. No one had dared open the doors leading out of the complex or they would have let in the burning heat.

And the older people died and the younger ones took their place. The shelter was designed to recycle food and air and water and remain eternally self-sufficient. This was their only home and thoughts of the outside had become pleasant memories marred by the imagination's picture of the effects of the burning heat. Then these memories had faded into legend as generation succeeded generation and still the bells never rang.

Maybe in those early days some unfortunate woman had given birth to a handicapped child. Desperate to avoid mutation in a closed environment, artificial rerproduction had been decreed, so that every birth could be guaranteed pure by laboratory tests and controls. But in order to do that they had had to kill the sexual urge. Which had proved impossible. Even after all this time, with the bells still silent, the need of man for woman and of woman for man was still alive.

But surely the radiation hazard must have lessened over so long a period? The bells must have been designed to go off automatically whenever it dropped below a certain level of danger.

He was considering the implications of this when he rounded a sharp bend in the tunnel and reached the open air.

It was still fairly dark, because the mouth of the tunnel was completely covered with vegetation, and he had to hack and stamp his way through it to get right outside. And when at last he stood beyond the branches covering the tunnel and looked round he knew the answer.

There had never been a nuclear attack.

He glanced at his wrist geiger yet again, but the needle had refused to move anywhere near the danger zone.

Trist took a deep breath and opened his face plate. There was a sweet lush scent of midsummer flowers

153

and growth in his nostrils. A gentle breeze rustled the branches of the trees and bushes growing in wild profusion all round him. Somewhere a bird was singing, and the notes held a haunting sweetness. Slightly to his right he could see what looked like the remains of a building, but from here it was too covered with creepers and vines to be sure. If it was it looked as if it had simply crumbled through neglect rather than deliberate destruction. Further away there were other similar green-covered humps.

It could have been a town, and he looked round to try to get his bearings. Behind them, the tunnel mouth was let into the side of a hill, and as he followed the lie of the land he felt recognition stir in him. It looked very like one of the three hills where his ship had been buried, but he was viewing it from a strange angle.

And what was more natural than that? He had been found when the tunnel was being excavated and taken down to the shelter below, and now he had emerged again, he had no idea how much later.

An insect droned lazily past him. It was high summer, and the planet's primary was blazing down from a late evening sky of high golden cloud. Everywhere was the lushness of vegetation run riot, of thigh length grass and enormous trees bearing heavily laden branches. Wild flowers grew all around his feet and in the bushes he had pushed through to get out. He knelt down and picked one.

It was a delicate bloom with five pink petals and a golden centre, very small and dainty, and it seemed to nod to him in a friendly fashion in the breeze.

He turned reluctantly and forced his way through the bushes again, heading back into the tunnel and the underground complex.

As he made his way downwards towards the first of the vast doors sealing the complex from the beautiful world outside questions were already clamoring for answers.

If there had been no nuclear attack, why had the bells which the people expected not rung? Why had there been no rescue from the surface? Why, finding the world so clean and pure, had people like Jennifox not returned with the glad news? And furthermore, if there had been no nuclear attack, why had the civilization above the ground deteriorated to the point of non-existence?

Only a small proportion of the population would have been able to take shelter underground.

What had happened to all the rest?

7

Selena gazed incredulously at the elders facing her on the platform. She was isolated in the middle of the amphitheater, and the people had gathered round the walls. This sort of event was comparatively rare and there was bewilderment in their faces.

She had known it would happen, but somehow she hadn't thought of it happening when her Lord wasn't there. But he had left her to go to the burning heat and she was left alone to face the consequences of what they had done in his apartment.

Not that she regretted that action. The memory of it was very dear to her and her one regret was that now it could never be repeated. It would be a beautiful memory until she grew very old and useless and she was put to sleep and her body sent for reconstitution.

She had returned from the far limits of the world to be met by a messenger from the Medical Section, asking her to go immediately for examination. Ironically she had been summoned at that point because it was known that the Lord had gone away somewhere and it would be most convenient for her to undergo the examination while he would not have need of her services.

And of course the result was a foregone conclusion.

As she lay naked on the couch she had felt an unaccustomed distaste at the doctor's examination of her private parts. This had never worried her before, but now she felt that no one had rights there except her Lord. The doctor had shaken his head unhappily and the elders had been summoned and the trial fixed, and now here she was awaiting sentence. They wasted no time on these occasions, in case the culprit contaminated others, and she knew that what was to follow would be the worst of all, for they would insist on her telling who had mated with her.

Where was her Lord now? Eaten up by the burning heat Outside, no doubt, and her heart cried out in pain at the thought.

Fardon was pronouncing sentence. She was scarcely listening, for she knew what the sentence was. It had been driven into her for as long as she could remember by the abbess elder of the temple.

" . . . in solitary confinement in the Medical Section until it can be finally ascertained whether or not you have conceived," Fardon was saying, his voice heavy with sorrow. "If the result is positive you will be aborted at the earliest possible moment to prevent the possibility of monsters coming amongst us. It is evident that the drugs have proved ineffective on you, and therefore the dosage will be doubled in order to prevent the act from happening again. It now remains for us to discover who performed it with you, in order that he may be similarly treated and our world made secure once more. Who was the man?"

Selena shook her head. She couldn't tell them. She couldn't betray her Lord. Whatever they did to her her Lord's beauty and potency must never be impaired. It

156

was too great a joy to be thrown away, even if she herself should never experience that joy again.

"I shan't tell you, Fardon," she said defiantly, and there was a murmur of astonishment round the well-filled amphitheatre.

"The truth drugs will ensure that we will discover his name."

"I know. You can force me to tell you. But I shan't tell you willingly."

The murmur was suddenly drowned by a voice.

"But I shall," it said. "It was me."

She whirled round with a little unbelieving cry, and there he was, tall and beautiful in his godlike suit, striding towards her across the floor of the amphitheatre, his helmet in his hand.

She looked at him intently and felt her anxiety and her sense of isolation drain away.

"The Lord is not burned," she said wonderingly.

He smiled at her, that smile which made her heart and limbs turn to water and left her curiously weak. "No, Selena," he said softly. "I have been Outside and I am not burned."

He held out his hand to her and she reached out hesitantly to take what he offered.

It was tiny and delicate and of such pristine beauty that she caught her breath at the wonder of it. Its colours seemed to glow in her hand and a slight scent came from it which twisted her heart with a nameless longing.

"What is it?" she asked.

"It is a flower, Selena," he said. "It grows Outside. There are millions of them there and they are very beautiful."

"Millions like this?" she asked incredulously.

"Like that and many other kinds."

She looked at it for a long time and then, without quite knowing why, she slowly lifted her hands and pushed the flower into the dark depths of her hair.

"They haven't hurt you?" he asked, and she shook her head. He smiled in evident relief and turned to the elders standing watching from the platform.

"Fardon," he said. "I have returned from Outside."

There was another murmur round the ampitheater, this time one tinged with fear. Fardon looked round hastily at the other elders and then back at Trist.

"That is not possible, Lord," he said.

"Yes, it is," said Trist, and he took Selena's hand and she stood listening happily to him as he told the elders about Outside and the fact that there was no burning heat. She did not follow everything he said. It was enough that he had returned, bearing this beautiful gift for her, and now she could accept that an Outside which produced anything like the flower he had brought her could never be evil and monstrous.

Trist was switching his talk to questions now, questions which Fardon was trying to answer.

"How many times have Naturals been produced, Fardon?" he asked.

Fardon conferred with a stout female elder on his left for a moment.

"Our records show that in the last fifty years twenty-nine Naturals have been produced."

"Which means that many, many more must have been produced in the past."

"That is possible, Lord."

"And how many monsters have you had to destroy?"

"None, Lord," said Fardon immediately.

"I knew it," said Trist. "There have never been monsters. And why? Because there has never been any burning heat to create them."

"I think, Lord," said Fardon very firmly but with great respect, "that your reasoning is wrong, if you do not object to me saying so. The lack of monsters is surely due to the vigilance of our Medical Section in preventing their coming and to the healthy world in which we live."

They argued on and Selena lost the thread of it, and didn't really care. Her Lord had come back to her. That was all that mattered.

"There is much to be discovered," said Trist, "but what I want to tell you is this. The way to Outside is open. I will not force you to go. That decision must be yours. But you have a tradition that when I awoke I would lead you out of your troubles. This is the way I am doing it. It may not be an acceptable way to you, but it is there for anyone who wishes to follow. I admit I don't understand what happened to people Outside, though I think it is more likely that there was some form of attack other than by nuclear weapons. Perhaps some form of biological warfare which decimated the population but left the environment intact. If that was the case it might explain why your bells never rang. The radiation level had never risen, so the alarm was never set. If the alarm was never set it would never go off, because there had never been a danger in the first place . . ."

"I do not follow your arguments, Lord," said Fardon, and although she loved to listen to her Lord talk Selena felt a sneaking sympathy for the Chief Elder. "But you place us in a difficult position," Fardon went on, the tone of his voice unhappy. "Our laws are very strict on this point. The girl Selena is a Natural and we can never allow Naturals to produce children. For a Natural to have a Natural child would double the dangers of producing a monster. Abortion must be performed if she has conceived, and I must ask you to submit to the operation which ensures impotency."

Selena squeezed his hand and felt an answering pressure. When Trist spoke he seemed totally unconcerned.

"I won't submit to it because I'm not staying here," he said.

"We cannot let you go, Lord," said Fardon, almost with a pleading note in his voice.

"I have been Outside. The flower I brought proves it. And if you believe in the burning heat you must also believe anyone touching me will be infected by it. That is up to you. I am returning to the Outside and I am taking Selena with me. If she will come."

"I will come, Lord," she said immediately.

"I'm glad," he said as he drew her to him. "And remember. The way is open. Anyone who wishes can go Outside without danger."

Then he gently guided Selena towards the corridor, and the crowd fell back from them uncertainly as they headed for the barrier.

8

Trist hoped the sun would have set by the time they reached the surface. He was worried about the effect the open air would have on someone who had never experienced it before. He did not wish to upset Selena any more than she had to be upset, and she had undergone much since he had first met her less than a day of this world's time ago.

He wondered if the moon was visible just now. It would be a help if they could emerge in moonlight which he had told Selena about and which had seemed to fascinate her.

He held her close as they stumbled up the tunnel in the light of his helmet lamp. She was shivering uncontrollably and clinging to him as though he might disappear if she let go and leave her to face unknown and unknowable perils.

He had left the airlock doors open behind him. He was sure they would be discovered soon, and he hoped that curiosity would overcome the inevitable panic which would ensue when the die-hards amongst the underground complex assumed that the burning heat was getting in. It should not be long before the hardier spirits began to emerge from the tunnel.

They reached the turning which he knew led to the overgrown opening and he stopped.

"We are almost Outside now, my darling," he said. "You must be brave. I don't know how light it will be, but it may be so bright that it will hurt your eyes. I would go forward alone to find out, but I think you would rather stay with me."

She nodded, her face pale in the glow from his lamp, but her eyes trusting.

"If you would like to close your eyes until I tell you to open them then do so."

"I will keep them open, Lord," she said. "It will be easier that way."

He bent forward and kissed her, a difficult thing to do with his helmet on. Her mouth seemed a little dry, and he did not delay but took her hand again and led her round the corner.

As he pushed aside the overhanging bushes and led her through he realised he had chosen well.

It was night outside. An almost full moon glowed high above them, and the night was filled with the balmy luminosity of midsummer.

Selena stood wide-eyed, her fear evaporating as the quiet beauty of their surroundings touched her. A little breeze stirred her hair and she put up a hand to her cheek.

"The air is pushing me," she said with a world of wonder in her voice.

The outlines of the crumbled buildings were dim and indistinguishable in the moonlight, the shadows were deep and the stars winked down from an almost clear sky.

"The moon?" she asked, wrinkling her eyes as she looked directly at it.

"Yes," he said. "Your moon, Selena."

She smiled at him a little uncertainly.

"Perhaps I knew this," she said. "It is strange and yet not strange. I know it and yet I don't know it."

He felt chilly fingers running along the ridges of his spine. How was it that she had awakened echoes of a feeling almost exactly the same in him? Memories of meeting Prudence Briggs in the moonlight were fresh and overlaid on something much deeper, more basic and elemental. The moon was not strange.

And Haven had no satellite.

"I am glad you brought me, Trist," she said, and the thought which he had been trying to pursue was diverted for a moment.

For the first time she had used his name as he had asked her to do. At last he was no longer a being to be reverenced, but a person to share things with as an equal. The false disparity was gone and they were a man and a woman alone together.

He removed his helmet, took her by the shoulders and kissed her.

"You are very brave, my love," he said.

"Your suit is very bulky," she murmured softly, keeping her face close to him. "I cannot feel you in it. Trist, it is good to lie together in the Outside?"

"Very good," he said.

"Then shall we do it? I have an overwhelming urge to feel you inside me again."

He laughed in pure delight. Her frank uninhibitedness was as refreshing as the mildness of the air and the softness of the moonlight.

She began to work at the fastenings of his suit and he helped her, cursing the intricacies of the locks and seals which kept him in a closed environment.

When she had undressed him she stood back and

undid the belt round her tunic, and then with a graceful gesture of total abandon she stripped off the tunic itself and stood for a moment, letting the moonlight glow palely on the perfect contours of her body, feeling the wind caressing her, shivering with a sensual pleasure at the warm night breeze on her naked flesh.

"Oh, Trist," she said as he took her in his arms and he felt the gentle pressure of her breasts on him. "This is so good."

"It's going to be better," he said.

"Yes," she murmured breathlessly. "Much, much better."

9

By morning they had skirted the hill and Trist had found his bearings. The ship should lie not very far away, although the wood which had hidden it was no longer a landmark, for the whole area was covered with dense undergrowth.

As the light strengthened, Selena kept glancing over her shoulder to the place where the glow was beginning in the sky. Trist watched over her, ready to help and comfort her if the strength of the coming sunlight should prove too much. He had explained what the sun was, and that she must not look directly at it, but that its warmth was good and caused things to grow, like the flowers which had fallen forgotten from her hair during the night.

When the first bright arc appeared over the horizon Selena gasped and turned away, her eyes hunted, burying her face in his chest as the nearest and most comforting shelter from the searching light.

He spoke soothingly to her as the morning grew around them, and eventually persuaded her to look, not at the sky, but at the flowers growing on the ground. They had opened their petals, turning themselves towards the source of light and heat and she drew comfort from their delicacy and grace and was able to accept thereafter the enormity surrounding her.

He let her take her time. There was no need for hurry, although he had an urgent desire to find his ship. Not that it would be any use to him. It was out of commission and would remain so. Whatever happened the scout ship would never leave the ground again. It would remain for ever buried in the hillside beside Greet's grave.

But over the past day a crazy, illogical idea had been growing in his mind. The more he thought of it the more he realised it couldn't be true, and yet there were so many isolated things which connected to support the theory.

The moon was not strange.

The language which he understood.

Haven, the name of his home.

His love for Selena.

He did not pretend to know all the answers but these basic things combined to convince him that *this planet was home*.

How, he did not know. Maybe he would never know. But it had never seemed strange or alien in any way. Even as he had hurtled towards it in the crippled scout ship he had felt no real worry that this place might be inimical to survival. Some deep racial instinct had recognized it and accepted it, as the same instinct had recognized and accepted the moon, something which Haven did not have. Haven . . . a name which implied refuge . . .

It was right. He knew it was right. But how and why he could not fathom and he found himself tantalized by the additional questions which this theory had given rise to.

By the configuration of the hills he found his way to the place where the scout ship had been buried. They

164

must have walked right through the Town Complex to get here but there was little to see except for a few moss and lichen covered walls. The marks of civilization had very quickly worn away.

He might not have found the exact spot where the ship lay buried had it not been for the thick screen of bushes which hid the tunnel mouth very much as the bushes had hidden the tunnel from which they had emerged.

And there it lay, just inside and to the right of the entrance. He pulled aside the bushes for Selena to follow behind him, and he felt an odd sense of comfort when he first caught the silver glimmer of the hull.

The ship lay canted at an angle, lying on solid rock, half covered by earth falls from the walls of the tunnel and the erosion of the years. Weeds were growing profusely as though trying to hide it. The hatch had been torn out of the ship, presumably to reach him when it had been discovered, but apart from that there seemed to be no further damage.

With tools from the emergency pack Trist began to clear away the overhanging branches and expose the ship so that the batteries could receive power from the sunlight.

He was not quite sure why he did this. Perhaps it was a natural thing to wish to restore the ship as much as he could. Some time later it lay exposed again, its solar reflectors soaking up power. Trist and Selena sat in the couches, the viewports transparent, and he explained the workings of the ship to her in terms as simple as possible. He switched on the radio, setting the thousand-year-old distress signal working again, and told her that with this machine he had been able long ago to talk to people far away in other worlds.

At this she snorted disbelievingly.

"I don't see how you can talk to people when you can't see them," she said.

He tried to explain the principles of radio to her, but she seemed unable to grasp them.

"Anyway, I don't hear anyone talking on *that*," she said conclusively. "You're not talking to *them*, and certainly no one's talking to *you*."

"It's broadcasting a continuous distress call," said Trist.

"Then why isn't anyone answering it?"

He smiled a little wryly.

"Because there isn't anyone to answer it now," he said.

He sat looking at the radio and the speaker which remained silent, his thoughts far away.

"This poor creature knows nothing and is humble in her ignorance," said Selena, "but I think the Lord is speaking through a hole in his helmet."

He turned sharply to her, about to deny it indignantly, when he stopped himself in time. She was looking at him out of the corner of her eye, her lips trembling with suppressed laughter, and his indignation vanished.

"Do you know what they do on my world to girls who are impertinent?" he asked.

She turned to him, her eyes wide with a knowing innocence.

"No, Lord. What?" she asked.

"This," he said, and he grabbed her and pulled her over his knee and drew up her tunic and slapped the delicious convexities of her bare bottom with a gentle hand. She relaxed in apparent submission.

"Oh, the Lord is so strong and violent," she said, her voice shaking with laughter.

He knew what she was doing. She was taking his mind off old useless memories, trying to prevent the black pall of depression from settling on him. And she had succeeded. The depression had gone.

166

"Do they do this in your world too?" he asked, giving her another slap.

"No. It's too dangerous. Even with the drugs it might excite people too much."

"I should have thought that was highly likely," he said.

"I have noticed you are sometimes excited by my bottom." she said conversationally. "Does it excite you now?"

"Yes, it does."

"I am glad. Because I am excited too and I think it would be a good thing if we lay together again."

"Woman, you're insatiable."

"Yes, Trist, I am. I have to make up for lost time."

He laughed and pushed her off him and she scrambled out of the scout ship on to the grass outside. He followed her, content to play the game with her. There seemed nothing else to do in any case. He had achieved his object. He was back at the ship with her. He had no idea what further progress there might be and for the moment he was prepared to lay it aside as unimportant.

She held out her hand to him and he took it and picked her up in his arms. He carried her towards a grassy bank outside the tunnel and she nuzzled close to him and bit his ear.

And then two things happened at once.

Something struck him a violent blow on the reinforced joint at the left shoulder of his suit, and looking down he saw a thin metal shaft fall to the ground. If it had struck an inch higher or lower it would have penetrated the suit and him too.

Before he had time to realise the implications a voice, harsh and metallic with distort and static, came from the scout ship.

"Trist," it said sharply. *"This is Captain Graud. Where the hell are you, man?"*

In that timeless moment so much seemed to happen that Trist afterwards was never able to piece things together in quite the right order.

The most important thing was that somewhere, something had attacked them with the clear intention of killing them. Here they were totally exposed, and the stun gun was in the ship. He turned with Selena in his arms and raced back to the shelter of the tunnel mouth.

He slid behind the ship which lay partly across the tunnel entrance. It was a fine natural defensive position. If he lay on the ground there was a gap between the ship's hull and one of the bent engine fins where he could cover any approach from outside. He put Selena down and she staggered and swayed slightly and put a hand to her shoulder. His heart missed a beat when he saw blood ooze gently between her fingers, and he suddenly filled with thoughts of Prudence Briggs . . .

The missile which had struck him must also have struck her and she had not been protected . . .

"Let me see," he said.

"It's all right," she said, her voice trembling a little with shock. "Who—who did that, Trist?"

"I don't know. They may attack again. Listen, my darling, stay down here. I'll give you a gun. If they should attack, you can hold them off, whoever they are. I'll get the first aid box . . . Let me see."

She took her hand away and he looked at her shoulder. Relief spread through him when he saw that it was only a flesh wound.

"We'll have to do something about that." he said.

"It isn't bad, is it, Trist?" she asked anxiously.

"No," he said. "But I don't want you to have a scar

on your shoulder for the rest of your life."

She smiled at him a little shakily.

"Maybe we shall lie together later," she said hopefully.

"You have a one track mind," he said as he jumped from the hatch and pulled himself into the cabin.

"Does that upset you?" she asked, and he grinned briefly. She was all right.

He found the stun gun in the locker, and threw it down to her.

"If anyone appears, point that at him and pull the trigger," he said.

She nodded and picked up the gun, examining it gingerly.

He pulled out the first aid kit and was busy searching through it for an antiseptic cream when the radio boomed again.

"Trist, come in," said the voice of Captain Graud. *"What the blazes is going on?"*

Strangely he had scarcely thought of that unexpected voice. It was as though with its sudden appearance the last few pieces were slipping into place. Captain Graud and the *Revelation* still existed *here* and *now,* and the whole shape of his theory was suddenly plain before him. He understood. It was all logical and right.

He picked up his helmet and slipped it over his head, switching the radio from automatic to direct.

"Captain, this is Trist. Where are you?"

"Damn it, Trist, I asked first. Where are *you?*"

"I'm on a planet. The primary has a system of nine planets. I'm on the third one out. It has a single large satellite . . ."

"Suffering stars, so are we . . . ! What . . . ? All right, let's have it . . ." This last was muffled as Captain Graud spoke to someone beside him. "Right. Trist. We've got a fix on you. What's your status report?"

"The ship's badly damaged, Captain. We're in

trouble. We've just been attacked. I don't know who by . . ."

"Bow and metal arrow?" snapped Graud.

"Something like that."

"Those are the Nomads. How long have you been there?"

Trist grinned. This was going to cause a sensation.

"In this planet's time?" he asked.

"Yes, if you like," said Graud testily. "Just give us *something, something*, will you?"

"I'm not sure," said Trist. "But I think it would be somewhere in the region of three thousand years."

There was silence and Trist could almost see the incredulity on the faces of the crew and the anger building up in Graud's broad face.

"Look here, Trist, are you drunk or something?" he barked.

"No, Captain. I'll explain it to you when you get here."

"It had better be good," rumbled Graud. "It's less than a year Earth time since you were lost. All right. I'm coming over myself in the second scout ship. Be with you in an hour."

"All right, Captain. We need help pretty badly, I think."

"You and Greet should be able to hold off a bunch of Nomads with bows and arrows," said Graud scornfully.

"I forgot to tell you. Greet's dead."

"What?"

He died when the meteor struck us."

"You said *we*. Who have you got with you?"

"A girl. A girl from this planet. A different group from the Nomads."

"Now look here, Trist, I don't want you fooling around with any of these people. Not till I've seen you, anyway. You know the laws about fraternizing with aliens."

"Yes, Captain. But these people aren't aliens, are they?"

There was another pause.

"How the bloody hell did you find that out? You'd disappeared before we had the briefing."

"You forget I've been here a long time, Captain," said Trist.

There was silence again except for heavy breathing.

"I'm on my way," snapped Captain Graud. "The ship will be listening if you want any help."

There was a click and the speaker went dead.

Trist removed his helmet, gathered the antiseptic cream and a covering plaster and was jumping out of the hatch when he heard the phutt of the gun.

Selena was lying against the scout ship, looking through the gap he had shown her, and he flopped down beside her.

"This machine works, Trist," she said wonderingly, and nodded forward through the gap.

In the rocky clearing about twenty yards away lay a man. He was dressed in a rough coat of animal skin. His hair was long and he had a thick, matted beard. In his hand he held a curved piece of metal. He was unconscious.

"Keep watching," he said. "Let me see that shoulder."

With a piece of bandage he wiped away the blood, exposing a long superficial wound. He applied the cream, hearing her gasp a little at the sting, but she never took her eyes off the exposed ground in front of her. Then he pressed the covering plaster into place.

"That's it," he said. "In three days you'll be as good as new."

"Thank you, Trist," she said.

171

"How many of them have you seen?" he asked.

"Only that one, but there are several, I think. I have heard them talking amongst themselves."

"We'll have help in an hour."

He took the gun from her and glanced at the charge meter. The gun was almost empty. He had used it a lot in the Investigating Department room when he had escaped with Prudence, and that had been a long time ago. Another two or three shots and it would be useless and he had no spare charges . . .

"What was that voice, Trist?"

"That was the radio which you were being so rude about," he said lying beside her and keeping a careful watch on the view ahead of them. At the moment all seemed quiet.

"I thought that must be it," she said. "I did not understand. I'm sorry."

"Don't be."

"But I thought you said there was no one to answer it."

"I wasn't sure. It seemed impossible. Yet I wondered."

"Who did answer it, Trist?"

"The Captain of my ship."

"But—but you said—"

"That I had been here for three thousand years? I know. That was what puzzled me. It puzzles Captain Graud. But I think I know what happened."

There was a stir in one of the bushes fringing the clearing and Trist fired. At the same time there was a spurt of dust just ahead of them and one of the wicked metal arrows lay with its head buried in the ground, its tail and flights quivering. The bushes wavered for a moment and then another of the Nomads fell outwards and hit the ground, unconscious.

"That is a marvellous thing you have, Trist," she said. "It kills so silently."

172

"It doesn't kill. I've got it set to medium, which means that these men should stay unconscious for over an hour. But there are only two more shots. Perhaps three. I can't refill it."

She was silent while the implications hit her.

"Oh," she said, and there was silence again for a time. "You said you thought you knew what happened," she said at last.

He nodded, and while they lay watching in the shadow of the scout ship, he told her his theory.

Ships reaching the speed of light disappeared. This he knew. And till now none had reappeared. But his had. Three thousand years earlier.

When the scout ship went superlight it jumped through time. Backwards. Everyone knew there was some kind of barrier at the speed of light. So far as he knew no one had ever considered that it might be purely a time barrier. There was no reason why it shouldn't be. The fact that he had only been superlight for a short space of time perhaps meant that he had not travelled far back along the timeline. Other ships might not have been so lucky. They might have stayed superlight for much longer. Perhaps they might even have dropped through the beginning of time . . . His mind boggled at that concept and he avoided expounding it to Selena.

So he had jumped roughly three thousand years back. The speed of the ship and the difference in time could account for the strange and unfamiliar look of the stars when he re-emerged. And he had landed on this planet many years before the people had developed space travel and begun to journey to the stars . . . But when they had done, probably to escape the impending nuclear holocaust, they had found refuge on one star's planet and called it Haven.

"And that's it," he said. "It explains why I understand your language. It hasn't changed much from

173

the time my people left and your people went underground. But the important thing is that I couldn't love you, my darling, if you were from a different species."

"Yes, Trist. I have known this all the time. You and I are one. But why is it that you are so much bigger than we are?"

"Difference in gravity and atmospheric pressure on Haven would account for that over many generations."

She looked a little puzzled, and he realised that she had no knowledge of what gravity or atmospheric pressure meant, but she seemed content merely that he was content with an explanation.

"But if your ship was out of control and separated from your mother ship, and if the sky is as big as you say, I don't understand how you both end up on the same small—planet, as you call it."

He nodded.

"This worried me, but I think I can explain it—"

"Look out, Trist!" she called, and he followed her suddenly pointing hand. Well to the right a wavering in the tall grass showed where one of their attackers was trying to come in on their flank. Trist managed to bring the gun to bear and fired, but it was lucky that Selena had noticed the man, for if he had been a little closer he could have gained the cover of the tunnel wall. The wavering stopped suddenly, and Trist glanced anxiously at the gun. The needle had sunk to the zero mark.

He guessed that perhaps a little more than half an hour had gone since he had talked to Captain Graud, and the Nomads were closing in.

He made up his mind.

"Listen, my darling," he said. "I'm going out to them."

She whirled round, her eyes wide with fear.

"No., Trist!" she said. "Don't leave me."

"It won't be for long," he said. "Maybe I can keep

174

them talking till the ship comes. But if we stay here it'll only anger them and we can't hold them off if they really want to get us. The gun's empty now, but they don't know that and they may be careful if they think we still have some defense. This way we have a chance."

"They'll kill you," she whispered.

"Perhaps, but I don't think so. The first arrow hit my suit and bounced off. I know it injured your shoulder, but it was meant for me, and they saw that it didn't go in. Maybe they'll think their arrows can't hurt me so they won't bother to fire."

She shook her head in violent disagreement.

"No, Trist, no—!" she pleaded, tears springing to her eyes.

But he knew he would have to go and there was no point in delaying.

"Stay here and wait. If the worst comes to the worst Captain Graud will look after you."

Before she could reply, and before the helpless, hopeless look in her face made him change his mind, he pushed the useless gun into her hand, slipped round the side of the scout ship and walked into the clearing beyond.

In spite of his confident words to Selena he felt terribly exposed. He held his hands out from his sides, open, to show that he had no weapon concealed, and he walked slowly to the middle of the clearing and stood facing the fringe of trees.

Hours seemed to drag by, hours during which his spine tingled in the expectation of an arrow between his shoulder blades.

But nothing happened.

Then after what seemed an eternity the bushes ahead of him parted and a man appeared and stepped cautiously into the open.

From his left came another man and from his right a

third. Trist felt sure there were more who remained hidden behind the thick foliage of the bushes.

For a moment he almost believed he had slipped back three thousand years and that once again he was standing in the clearing in the forest with the camp fires of the Picts around him. The men were only slightly bigger than the Picts had been, and their clothing was similarly coarse and unbecoming. They were as hairy and wild-looking, but their bodies were not painted, and the bows and arrows were made of a material which would have been unknown to the Picts. Where had these weapons come from . . . ?

"Greetings," he said. "Let us talk."

He watched the center man closely and saw recognition in his eyes at the language Trist used. The eyes were blue and piercingly intelligent and the man had understood his words. He grunted and then spoke. Trist had difficulty in making out what he said for the accent was terribly thick, but with concentration and occasional repetition the meaning became clear.

"You have a woman," he said.

Trist nodded.

"We want her," said the man.

"Why do you want her?" asked Trist evenly, though his heart had missed a beat.

"We need her for breeding."

"Suppose she doesn't want to come?"

"She will come."

"Suppose I won't allow her to go."

The men on either side raised their bows threateningly, but the man in the middle gestured impatiently and they lowered them again.

"I don't know who you are," he said, his blue eyes calculating and quick. "Clearly you are very strong and you are not one of us. We need women. You are a stranger and cannot know our need or you would not ask about this."

"Why do you need women?" Trist asked.

The man seemed prepared to talk, which was a good thing. He shrugged his shoulders.

"We have women. But they do not bear fruit. Very, very, few bear fruit."

Trist nodded. He had not been far wrong with his assumption of some sort of biological weapon instead of a nuclear one. A nuclear attack would have been violent and conclusive, but what had actually happened had been insidious and obscene. It had decimated the population left on the surface, and the few survivors had been unable to repair the damage caused by the loss of technology. And it had affected the women and made them barren. The few who could bear children would have a pretty severe time of it. He shuddered when he thought of Selena being used in this way, bearing a succession of children until her belly and breasts were flabby and worn, and the terrible prospect of a large group of men working out their lusts on her. That must have been what happened to Jennifox. Either willingly or unwillingly she would have been absorbed into the group.

"Your woman looks good for child-bearing," said the man. "We watched you last night."

Trist felt himself flushing and hoped that Selena could not hear.

"It is wrong that one man should have one woman. She must be taken into the group for the use of the group."

"And me?" asked Trist.

The man regarded him calculatingly.

"If your seed is implanted in the woman it will be allowed to grow. Your strength will help the race. But you are too big to trust. You might cause the group harm. We would have to kill you."

Trist nodded understandingly.

"And you think you can do that?" he asked.

177

For a moment the man hesitated.

"I think so," he said at last, but there was a note of uncertainty in his voice.

"Let me tell you a thing," said Trist. "I came from the sky. Many, many years ago. If you try to kill me, others will come from the sky and demand a reckoning. They are coming now and they will be here very soon. If you kill me, you will have to answer to them. If you leave me and the woman alone they will help you to do many things which you can no longer do."

The bowman glanced uneasily at the sky and then at their leader. He stood silently, assessing what Trist had said, and eventually he smiled coolly.

"It is a good story, man," he said. "but it is not true."

He snapped an order which Trist could not follow, and the two men flanking him suddenly raised their bows and drew back the strings. Trist saw the wicked pin-points of the arrows aiming straight for him.

"One in each eye," said the leader. "Your clothing is too thick to pierce. We shall see if your friends come from the sky to save you."

Trist squeezed his eyes tight shut as though that might prevent the arrows from penetrating. Strange coloured patterns formed in the darkness behind his eyelids, patterns which seemed suddenly beautiful. *Selena,* he thought, and wondered if there might be enough charge left in the gun for her to turn it on herself and make herself unconscious . . .

There was a sudden grunt and he opened his eyes. The men had lowered their bows and were looking beyond him. He whirled round and gasped.

Selena was walking towards them from the shelter of the scout ship.

"Go back!" he yelled. "Selena, you fool! Go back!"

But she came on. The white tunic contrasted with the

178

glow of flesh and the black hair, and the breeze blew the thin material against her, moulding the shape of her body. There was a strangely confident look on her face. She was safe from death from these men. They needed her alive, and therefore she had a certain bargaining platform. But at what a cost, he thought.

She stopped beside him and stood silently, staring at the three men. She looked proud and haughty and commanding and infinitely desirable. And she knew it. One thing she had clearly learnt from him was the beauty of her complete womanhood.

He felt himself awed but at the same time relieved. Till now he had been the dominant partner. It was not good that one should dominate too much. From now on they would be equals.

If there was a future for them.

"You will not touch the Lord," said Selena quietly, but with an authority in her voice which he had not heard before.

The men said nothing, but Trist noticed the leader watching her a little uncertainly.

"The Lord spoke truly," she said. "He came from the sky to save your people. And mine. This he has done. Today sees the meeting of all our people again, and together we shall go forward. If you wish I will go with you—"

"Selena—" Trist found his voice to protest, but she turned to him and the calm determination and authority in her face made him pause with the protest unuttered.

"Trust me," she said quickly. "As I am trusting you."

Her eyes flickered upwards towards the sky as she said it, and he realized that she too was waiting for Captain Graud's arrival, and that she was prepared to spin out time until the ship appeared.

She turned back to the men.

179

"If you wish to lie with me there is much to be arranged," she said. "If I were unwilling I could spoil your pleasure."

Trist scanned the skies with anxious eyes while Selena squatted on the ground and began to bargain. He listened with keen distaste to the conversation, but it seemed as though the bargaining was something these people understood and appreciated, and it might take some time.

Because he was listening for it, and knew what to listen for, he heard it first, the high-pitched whining just on the threshold of audibility which grew rapidly until the men heard it too and looked up with fear in their eyes.

"My friends are coming," said Trist.

The leader looked at him speculatively, and one of the guards gave a sudden cry and pointed.

High over the fringe of trees a silver glimmer grew and took shape, and Trist found his eyes watering as he recognised the familiar stubby lines of the second scout ship floating slowly downwards, its rocket fins pointing to the ground, the rumble of its braking engines growing, shattering the peace of the land around. It had been a long, long time since he had last heard that noise.

The two guards were urging their leader to get away, and the leader was clearly in two minds about it. Trist laid a hand on his shoulder.

"Stay," he said. "My friends are good."

The leader glanced at him dubiously, but seemed to take comfort from his words. He growled something to the guards, and they fell silent as the scout ship, glinting blindingly in the sunlight, came down below the level of the trees and the engines died in a final rumble as it came to rest upright a short distance away.

Trist felt Selena's hand creep into his, and knew that

she too was feeling an awe at this appearance, as were the others.

The hatch clanged open and two men emerged and jumped to the ground. Trist waited where he was, keeping a wary eye on the two guards, but the men seemed to have forgotten their bows and arrows in the shock of seeing men appear from the sky.

The short, stocky figure of Captain Graud rolled towards them on bandy legs, incredibly familiar and unchanged.

And here, he thought, was the meeting of the ways. As they had parted, so they had come together again. The three parts of humankind had reassembled to make a whole.

11

"You'd have made life a lot easier for me if you'd told us earlier we were coming to Earth," said Trist.

"I don't like your tone of voice," barked Captain Graud. "We may have posted you missing, but you're still a member of the ship's crew."

"I'm nothing of the kind," Trist retorted. "I signed on for fifteen years. I've been here for three thousand, as near as makes no difference."

Captain Graud's fingers rasped across the stubble of his chin.

"H'm," he grunted. "You may have a point there. Anyway, I was under orders not to divulge our destination until we were within striking distance of the planet."

"In Haven's name, why?"

Captain Graud shrugged and grinned mirthlessly.

"A mixture of politics and psychology, my boy, and if you ask me, that's a damned dangerous mixture."

They were sitting in Captain Graud's tiny cabin on

the *Revelation,* and Trist had had a strange feeling since he had come aboard from the scout ship that here was familiarity and strangeness. To Graud it was familiar, to Selena everything was of an eye-boggling alienness, and somewhere he was sitting in the uncomfortable middle. He tried to dispel the feeling as he held Selena's hand and listened to Captain Graud.

The starships had left Earth over five hundred years before. In fact, as near as he could make out, Trist realised that the first of them must have lifted off only a year or so after he had left Prudence Briggs dead on the pavement in the Town Complex. So the second sleep pill had knocked him out for so long as the first. There had been desperate haste to ready the ships so that some of humanity might survive what appeared the inevitable holocaust.

Some of the ships had headed for Alpha Centauri and after a journey of over five years they had discovered Haven, one of Alpha Centauri's seven planets.

Contact had been maintained with Earth, but it had been slow and difficult over the distance, and after a while communications from Earth had dropped so suddenly that the people from the starships knew that the holocaust had happened. Some messages filtered through from the main underground shelters, but over the centuries these faded and eventually vanished.

The Planetary Council of Haven argued and discussed. The psychologists had thought it advisable to play down memories of Earth, both for the sake of the peace of mind of the people, and also so that there would be less chance of Earth's example being followed on Haven.

So the people forgot, and only misty folk memories remained in the subconscious. There was much to do on Haven to make that world habitable and self-supporting. But the Planetary Council did not forget,

182

and as generation succeeded generation, watch was kept on Earth, an anxious watch, a secret watch, and when the final messages faded and died the Planetary Council believed that Earth too must have died at last.

But they had to be sure. In the closely guarded records of the Planetary Council there were too many memories of Earth to be lightly discarded. Someone must go to see if the planet was indeed a scorched cinder. There was always a chance that there might be survivors, living in impossibly primitive conditions. The truth must be found and, if necessary, help sent.

So the *Revelation* set out. The Captain knew their destination, though he was not told of the situation on the planet to which he was heading, and indeed knew nothing of Earth's history. He had sealed orders which were to be opened only under certain circumstances. If the planet was clearly incapable of supporting life he was to swing round and head for home again, the orders unopened, and the Captain and crew would know nothing of the purpose of their visit. If the planet was habitable, the orders would be opened, and Captain Graud would tell the crew the shortened history of the planet contained in them. The ship would land and they would see what the situation was and, in particular, why communications had ceased.

"And that's what we were doing when you switched on your distress call again and scared the living daylights out of us," said Captain Graud. "We found the Nomads, same as you did. They're clinging to life very tenaciously. We're curing the barrenness. I'm glad. Clever folk. Very inventive. Those bows and arrows. Marvellous things. Very deadly too. Use old metal they find lying around. Including the external transmitter aerials from the underground complexes. No wonder communications ceased."

"I do not understand this," said Selena. "I have never heard of us sending messages Outside."

183

"Maybe only a few of the bigger complexes did so," said Captain Graud. "And maybe the others transmitted automatically without human help. I don't know. Anyway, we'd only got as far as establishing contact with the Nomads when you came through on the distress frequency. You've done more than us. We hadn't even suspected that people might still be living underground."

"I've had longer to do it," said Trist.

"True," said Graud thoughtfully. "We'll need to get the scientific boys on to this jump through time of yours. Sounds crazy, but I suppose it's feasible. Certainly it'd explain why ships disappear from our time line at the speed of light. And of course you jumped time but not space. You got to Earth because the scout ship was on the same trajectory to the solar system here as the *Revelation*. It was inevitable that you should reach this system."

Trist shifted uncomfortably in his seat. Somehow since the arrival of Captain Graud the whole perspective of his existence had altered. It was almost as if the intrusion of his own kind had caused a jarring note. Idealistically he wished he had been left alone with Selena, that the two of them might have gone on living together in this fruitful, almost deserted world. But the Nomads had come, and the ship had come from Haven, and there were people underground . . .

He got to his feet.

"I'm going outside," he said abruptly.

Selena stood up and then paused. He scarcely glanced at her as he made his way out of the cabin, and she looked at the door as it closed behind him, her face distressed.

"Leave him, m'dear," rumbled Captain Graud. "It'll be best for him to be alone. He has a lot to think about. Much to assess. It won't be easy for him."

"Then I should be with him," she whispered.

"In a little while," said Captain Graud with surprising gentleness. "In a little while."

12

The *Revelation* stood on a bare patch of ground where her engines had burnt away the vegetation when she landed. Although she stood half way round the globe from the scout ship the country looked very much the same. Overgrown, lush and riotously undisciplined.

Trist strode blindly through the undergrowth. There was an urgent helplessness in him and he felt if he could only walk, keep his limbs moving, the pure physical exercise might help him to see things clearly.

Where did he belong?

He came from Haven, and he had only left Haven five years ago. Yet he had been here for three thousand years. Which planet had the greater claim on his emotions? He felt he was being pulled in two different directions.

And there was Selena.

His place was on Haven, but could he take her there? Would she even want to go? Did *he* want to go? He felt as though he belonged there. All right. He had been here for three thousand years, but he had only been consciously aware of perhaps a month. Could the subconscious memory of the rest of that time and the race memory of this planet draw him back? Or was it only Selena?

And how in Haven's name could he have fallen so deeply in love with a girl he had never even clapped eyes on two days ago? Surely it needed longer than that to be certain. Time. What was time? Three thousand years seemed like a day, and a day seemed like three thouand years.

He sat on a rock and stared unseeingly across a great plain of waving grass which stretched until it met the blue of the sky, and the problems of the universe marched in solemn procession before his eyes.

She came to him as the sun was setting and his shadow stretched out massive behind him. He did not see her until she knelt beside him and put her arms on his knees.

"My poor Trist," she murmured, and he buried his face in the warmth of her hair and the pent up strain of the years burst. He sobbed unrestrainedly for the friends he had lost and found and for the friends he had found and lost, and for the wasted years which had never been, and the happy years he had never known.

The sun set in golden glory and the shadows deepened around them. They were alone in the wide land, the ship and the Nomads and the underground people and Captain Graud forgotten, and yet they were all there in the shadows, waiting and watching.

"What will you do, Trist?" she asked softly at last.

He shook his head and surreptitiously wiped his eyes, feeling a sharp sense of shame that he should have given way in front of her like this.

"I don't know," he said.

"Captain Graud wants you to stay," she said.

"Why?"

"Because he says there is a lot to be done. Oh, Trist, he's right. There's so much to do and only you can do it. There are three peoples to be brought together, and you are the only one who knows all three. The undergrounders need the drive of the Nomads, and the Nomads need the technology of the undergrounders, and each needs the help of your people from Haven, and Haven needs the undergrounders and the Nomads to help to restore Earth. And there's only one man who can coordinate all that effort and make it work. You. So Captain Graud says."

He looked at her as she sat on the rock beside him, the long slim fingers of one hand absently rubbing the

186

plaster on her shoulders, and she seemed suddenly to resolve into a sharper focus. Of course, that was it. He had a unique experience of the history and workings of both planets. The only person who had. He could stay here and yet maintain close contact with his own world.

"Yes," he said quietly. "That's right. There is much to do. But I can't do it alone. I'll need help."

"Captain Graud says he can let you have two or three men from the crew, and the Nomads are already willing to work with your people from Haven. I'm sure once the undergrounders start coming Outside they will want to join too. You will have plenty of help."

"Yes. I'm sure there'll be enough. But I need more than their help. I need yours as well."

"It is always there, Trist. I think we two can be the greatest help of all. We two from different worlds will be an example, perhaps."

"I hope so. Two people in equal partnership, Selena. If you will have me, I will stay."

She looked at him with twinkling eyes.

"Yes, Lord," she said, her voice trembling between laughter and tears. "Your humble servant will have you. In fact, I'd like to see anyone try to stop me."